T0113020

PRAISE FOR AGNES RAVATN

WINNER of the Norwegian Booksellers' Award
WINNER of the English PEN Translation Award
Shortlisted for the Dublin Literary Award
Shortlisted for the Petrona Award for Best Scandinavian Crime
Novel of the Year
Longlisted for the CWA International Dagger

'What a delightfully insightful and wicked little read ... it's so
minimalist and stark and at the same time so compelling. I see
that it's been compared to Christie, and I can see that in the
cleverness and the twists, but Agnes's writing also reminded me
so much of one of my all-time favourite authors, Orwell –
which is probably why I enjoyed it so much' Elizabeth Haynes

'*The Guests* is fast-paced and fascinating. This was a long-
awaited story from a very talented and original author. I was not
disappointed. Definitely recommended'
Jen Med's Book Reviews

'A quiet sort of book, but surprisingly fast-paced for such a
character-driven story. Every little detail, from Karin's issues to
the setting is pitch-perfect, and still there is something a little
off-key about the whole, which was somewhat unsettling. I had
a great time with *The Guests* – I was completely captivated. I
would recommend it to readers who enjoy their drama with a
good dose of psychology and psychological suspense' From
Belgium with Booklove

'A clever, quirky mystery, full of twists and reminiscent of
Agatha Christie at her best' *The Times*

'Ravatn, one of Norway's premier crime writers, manages to
conjure up an extra level of chilling atmosphere that will make
you want to put the heating on ... *The Seven Doors* packs a
brutal punch' *Sun*

THE GUESTS

ABOUT THE AUTHOR

Agnes Ravatn is a Norwegian author and columnist. She made her literary début with the novel *Week 53* in 2007. Since then she has written a number of critically acclaimed and award-winning essay collections, including *Standing*, *Popular Reading* and *Operation Self-discipline*, in which she recounts her experience with social-media addiction, and how she overcame it.

Her debut thriller, *The Bird Tribunal*, won the cultural radio P2's listener's prize in addition to The Youth's Critic's Prize, and was made into a successful play, which premiered in Oslo in 2015. The English translation, published by Orenda Books in 2016, was a WHSmith Fresh Talent Pick, winner of a PEN Translation Award, a BBC Radio Four 'Book at Bedtime' and shortlisted for the Dublin Literary Award and the 2017 Petrona Award for Best Scandinavian Crime Novel of the Year. Critically acclaimed *The Seven Doors* was published in 2020. Agnes lives with her family in the Norwegian countryside.

ABOUT THE TRANSLATOR

Rosie Hedger was born in Scotland and completed her MA (Hons) in Scandinavian Studies at the University of Edinburgh. She has lived and worked in Norway, Sweden and Denmark, and now lives in York where she works as a freelance translator. Rosie translated Agnes Ravatn's *The Bird Tribunal* and *The Seven Doors* for Orenda Books, and her translation of Gine Cornelia Pedersen's *Zero* was shortlisted for the Oxford-Weidenfeld Translation Prize 2019. Follow Rosie on Twitter @rosie_hedger.

Also by Agnes Ravatn
and available from Orenda Books

The Bird Tribunal
The Seven Doors

THE GUESTS

Agnes Ravatn

Translated by Rosie Hedger

Orenda Books
16 Carson Road
West Dulwich
London SE21 8HU
www.orendabooks.co.uk

First published in Norwegian as *Gjestene* by Det Norske Samlaget, 2022
First published in English by Orenda Books in 2024
Copyright © Agnes Ravatn, 2022
English translation copyright © Rosie Hedger, 2024

ISBN 978-1-913193-58-4
eISBN 978-1-916788-00-8

This book has been translated with financial support from NORLA

Typeset in Garamond by typesetter.org.uk

Printed and bound by CPI Group (UK) Ltd, Croydon CR0 4YY

For sales and distribution, please contact info@orendabooks.co.uk

THE GUESTS

The archipelago elite grew closer with every right turn. Effortlessly well-turned-out, nut-brown couples appeared on the horizon, one after another, increasing in number as we approached our destination. Our orange van made for a clownish addition to the black electric SUVs.

We eventually turned onto a narrow gravel track that ended without warning at the edge of a towering precipice.

Here, then? Kai said, turning off the engine as I looked up from the map on my phone and out at the view before us.

This was the land of soft, smooth, coastal rocks, worn away over twelve thousand years.

This must be it, I said.

Neither of us even wanted to stay at the stupid cabin in the first place. For once, my in-laws had invited our boys to stay over at theirs, and Kai had booked the entire week off work. I had been completely prepared to spend the week taming the garden while he finally finished work on the decking – ten years after we'd bought the house.

I wasn't a fan of the archipelago lifestyle; it simply wasn't for me. Never had been. I was too burdened by self-reflection, too exhausted, too uncomfortable in my own skin and in the clothing I wore, as if I should be wearing someone else's – not that I had any notion of whose.

Kai, on the other hand, was adaptable.

When I told him we'd be staying in a cabin rather than working on the garden, for example, and not only that, but that I'd also got him a job, he'd reacted with only mild surprise.

It's a paid holiday! I'd said, typing the cabin's location into the map on the iPad, a grey rooftop nestled among the white rocks and sparse vegetation, I zoomed in so close that we could see the benches and huge stone table in the outdoor seating area.

Some of us have to work on this so-called holiday, he said.

But it's so close to the sea! I'd said. And hardly another cabin to be seen anywhere nearby!

But Karin, I thought we'd agreed... he began, but when I zoomed in on the white boat he trailed off mid-sentence, and I could practically see him making a mental list of all the extra fishing gear he would have an excuse to buy.

That was Kai all over, ready to turn anything into a positive, much more so than I ever could, a fact that he was always keen to highlight.

We took our luggage – Kai with his nautical-looking canvas bag, me with my impractical, unsuitable suitcase on wheels – and lugged them along a dry path that wove its way through the natural vegetation, great tufts of sea thrift tucked between tall, tough, shiny blades of grass, until we made it onto the smooth coastal rocks. I'd only ever seen rock formations like this in pictures; there were pink and orange and brown hues amidst the grey, rippling and rolling before us, almost soft underfoot.

Water appeared up ahead, a view of what surely had to be Skagerrak strait – was that the ocean or the sea? – and I stopped in my tracks.

Such a shame, I said, shaking my head. Detonating a pathway through an untouched natural landscape like this, just to create a holiday paradise for the well-heeled.

Kai looked at me.

I don't think anyone's been detonating anything around here, have they? he said.

In general, I mean, I replied, hauling my suitcase behind me.

I felt a creeping sense of discomfort as I approached the

spot where Iris Vilden's cabin was said to be located. I took
in the view. A gentle, salty breeze and the predictable
screeching of gulls, but no sign of any cabin. According to
the blue dot on my phone we were here, standing right
beside it. It occurred to me that the whole thing had been
one big practical joke, that there was no cabin, that Iris was
sitting at home giggling away to herself, but then I heard Kai
shouting: Over here!

He was standing on a rock ten metres ahead of me. I
climbed up to join him and immediately caught sight of
the cabin. It was nestled perfectly within a natural dip in
the rock, beneath two huge, rounded boulders and behind
five low, windswept pines, barely visible from any other
angle besides the one from which I was looking at that
moment.

Wow, Kai murmured as we made our way down a flight
of steps cast in concrete between two boulders.

The cabin wasn't as showy and vulgar as I'd hoped it might
be, in fact, it was tasteful and understated, constructed from
greying wood, glass and natural stone.

Well, this is, hmm, I said, unable to think of anything to
say. I'd been anticipating something a little more offensive
and garish, easier to find fault with. There was nothing here
for Kai and I to ridicule and mock, at least not at first glance,
nothing we could exploit in order to strengthen our own

bond, only a wealth of environmentally friendly materials and extreme privilege.

A week here, I thought to myself, and already I felt drained, a week!

Kai ambled onto the patio and placed his bag on the table – a monstrous stone block balanced on two smaller ones – then turned to look out at the sea and took a deep breath in through his nose.

Inviting us out here was an attempt on Iris Vilden's part to provoke a bout of jealous self-reflection: why couldn't I even *imagine* such a cabin when she was in a position to *own* one?

I picked up my phone once again, opened the app to unlock the door and pulled up the code she'd sent me. I typed it in. The door clicked abruptly.

The inside of the cabin was more like a Scandinavian interior-design showroom than a holiday home for actual, real-life people.

I stepped into the cool hallway.

Wow, I mean, this must be worth what, twenty, thirty million kroner? I said slowly.

At least, Kai said.

How on earth were they even allowed to build this place? I asked.

They must have bought an old shack and sought planning

permission to demolish it and build another in its place, he said.

But I mean, this is a *conference centre*, I said.

I'm going to take a walk and check out the jetty, Kai said, before turning around and walking out.

You've become so blasé about these things, I called after him. He'd worked on so many fancy cabins in and around the Oslo fjord that nothing impressed him these days.

It was silent inside the cabin itself, in contrast to the gusts and the screeching of the gulls outside. The pale floor gleamed at me, they were the widest floorboards I'd ever laid eyes on.

Kai's silhouette passed the enormous window that looked out over the water; it wasn't a window, not really, more like a transparent wall.

I parked my suitcase in the middle of the room and took in the space around me.

It had light-coloured wood-panelled walls, and these had been adorned with what I could only describe as modern art, stuff that went over my head.

A three- or four-metre-long dining table with a vast tabletop of what had to be oak, filled the space. Ten matching chairs, no doubt all crafted by hand. In the corner by the sofa a huge, glass-fronted wood-burning stove.

I turned around to take in the kitchen. The cabinet doors

had been crafted from the same wood as the pale, oiled floorboards, not the kind of thing you could buy off-the-shelf from any old kitchen showroom.

A half-metre-wide, mirrored-chrome espresso machine took centre stage on the black stone worktop. There was a gas hob, an oven, what could have been a combi steamer, and a third unidentifiable type of oven, all stacked on top of one another. All of this for a *cabin*?

Kai and I had actually decided not to bother with a holiday this year. Kai was keen to squeeze in as much work as possible; the building trade was experiencing a bit of a slump, everyone was holding off on doing any building work due to the rise in costs. Rather than tackling the major work, people were ticking off the small building projects, and his phone never stopped ringing.

But the fact was that we had less cash to splash, in spite of the fact that we both worked full-time and never spent very much.

While it seemed that other parents in the area met Maslow's hierarchy of needs for their children without issue, providing endless hoodies and pairs of shoes and pieces of ski equipment, the prices of which were inversely proportional to the ever-decreasing number of snowy days each year, Kai and I were forced to pinch the pennies.

I felt as if I was here under duress, it weighed on me like

a heavy mass. I wanted to turn around. To drive home and send Iris a message to say that something had come up. But then it struck me that she could probably see from the door-locking app that we'd already arrived, and was no doubt waiting to hear from me to that effect.

There was only one picture in the entire cabin that wasn't an artistic abstract, the only indication that real people resided here, and it was a photograph on the wall between the bathroom and the master bedroom. A family of four photographed against the setting sun. Two small, tanned boys around the same age as my own, with big white grins and grains of sand on their shoulders, the wind-swept hair of surfers, bleached white by the sun and thick with saltwater.

Iris beamed in an exaggerated fashion; she was wearing a white bikini top, with her left arm disappearing out of shot behind the camera.

Standing in the house behind them was their father, a tall man in a basic, white T-shirt with a cap on his head backwards and sun-bleached hair sticking out each side, his face clean-shaven. A smug, masculine smile into the camera, two long, strong arms, she'd found the male version of herself. All of a sudden, I was overcome with fury at the fact the world is just like she is: how can it be that waiters, for instance, take one glance at my children and me and somehow intuitively understand that we don't deserve the same level of service as Iris and her children, how is it that they can decipher the tiniest of signs, the quality of our clothing, our haircuts, our complexions! – and why do we just accept it all?

What's up? Kai asked, appearing behind me all of a sudden, I'd let out an impulsive, loud snort without realising it. I turned around to face him.

What exactly am I supposed to do out here? I asked him.

Come on down and take a look at the boat with me, he said excitedly.

I'm tired, I said.

You're just hungry, he said. I'll bring in the food shopping. He turned around and walked out.

The food shopping, I thought to myself. Sliced bread, butter, Kai's seedless jam, the kind kids like, plus ham, cheese, cucumber. All very lower-middle class. I took a deep breath, I couldn't, *wouldn't*, let Iris win by descending into this mire of self-pity.

I grabbed my phone and started writing a message to her.

We're here. What a lovely place! followed by a bog-standard smiley. As I reviewed my nonchalant message designed to belittle what was hers, I saw three little bubbles appear on screen, Iris writing a reply, then they vanished.

I sat down on the sofa, surveyed the panorama that expanded before me, and thought to myself that it would be good for me to spend this holiday trying to adopt Kai's uncomplicated approach to his position in this universe. He wasn't prone to envy, unlike me; he didn't instinctively compare himself with others, he was capable simply of observing things with interest, his head cocked to one side.

For me, this cabin held no value simply because it wasn't mine, it never could be, and it could not, therefore, offer me anything other than a greater sense of defeat regarding my lowly position in the food chain.

My phone vibrated, a poorly disguised expression of Iris's disgruntlement: *Great!*, followed by an aggressive emoji, a smiley face that looked as if it were howling with laughter or pain. I considered it a tiny triumph, stood up and made my way towards the kitchen, which was so stunning that it left me incapacitated. I decided to knock up some sandwiches for lunch.

I wouldn't go so far as to say that I actively *dreaded* the prospect of being reunited with Iris Vilden, but I had spent my adult life hoping, more or less subconsciously, to avoid bumping into her again.

During my first few years in Oslo, I'd looked up her address once a year or so, just to be sure that we wouldn't encounter each other.

She'd always lived in the city centre. I had always lived in the north-east of the city, and in the years that passed, I'd gradually moved further and further away from the centre, eventually ending up across the county line, settling in the neighbouring municipality of Nittedal, way down south in Skillebekk.

While Kai was a professional one-man-band with a niche skill, which was creating space-saving interior-design solutions – making use of jamb walls, built-in bookshelves and beds, and so on – and which had him whizzing up and down the entire east coast in his orange Ford Transit van filled with tools, I was confined, day in and day out, to the same office in Nittedal City Hall, where I had willingly ended up working as a consultant after completing my law degree, and where I had spent almost ten years advising on quality improvements and internal regulations, a role for which I felt both over- *and* underqualified.

I rarely found myself in Oslo city centre, so the threat of bumping into Iris Vilden was far from imminent.

Then, in May, Kai had surprised me with a pair of concert tickets. Mahler's *Symphony No. 3* had never been a real favourite of mine – quite the opposite, in fact – and our seats were some of the worst in the house, but none of that mattered, because Kai had made the effort to go online and order them for my birthday, and that in itself was more than enough of a gift for me.

And it's a funny thing. Two hours in the company of the Oslo Philharmonic and five different choirs, it does something to a person. It was a powerful experience. Even Kai felt it, sitting there awkwardly in his best jacket, his hair dishevelled, his face bristly with three days' worth of thick stubble. He stuck out like a sore thumb, thanks in no small part to his slightly wonky nose – the result of an accident at work many years ago – which made him look like something of an outlaw.

He was pale when we stepped outside afterwards. I need a drink, he said, and I felt the same way. We made our way to a pub on Rosenkrantz gate, where we had a pint, then one more.

And just as I was about to say that we ought to be making

our way home to relieve our babysitter from her duties, the door opened, cold air filtered into the pub, and the icy breeze ushered a high-spirited, carnivalesque troop inside.

I glanced at the door and froze. It was her.

Quick, I said to Kai, hide me!

He looked at me, puzzled.

Hide me! I repeated. He grabbed his coat and tentatively held it up like some sort of curtain, and I whispered, *We have to leave, NOW*. It was a spontaneous, natural reaction, instinctive, animalistic. The coat muffled the commotion in the pub as I tried to figure out an escape route.

By the bar, I whispered, and Kai pulled a face – what's going on? – as I carefully stood up. Kai picked up his glass and finished the contents before standing up beside me. I cleaved to the walls, treading carefully, it was a Friday night and the place was packed with boisterous, inebriated punters to hide behind, but out of the corner of my eye I realised that somehow, by some miraculous twist of fate, she had managed to catch sight of me, and we were summoned.

KARIN? she bellowed hoarsely from across the pub, and rather than pretending I hadn't heard her, I stopped as if on command. She slithered her way through the bustling crowds like a jaguar, cutting us off just as we reached the bar.

My God, she said, looping a tentacle around my wrist and drawing me in towards a cheek that sparkled with stage makeup. My God, it must be, what? – and I could see her unsuccessfully trying to guess how long it had been since we'd last seen each other.

Twenty-five years, I said.

My God, she repeated, her mouth agape, then she caught sight of Kai behind me, his coat now under his arm.

Have we met?

Oh yes, I said, this is...

Kai offered an outstretched hand. I'm Kai, he said, nice to meet you.

She was wearing some sort of black, floral, low-cut kimono, she turned around to look at me, her mouth still wide open.

We were just leaving, I said.

You don't want to come and sit with us? she asked, and she nodded in the direction of the group she'd arrived with. We're celebrating the opening night of my one-woman show at Oslo New Theatre.

Oh, wow, I said, congratulations.

Then a moment of silence.

In my naivety, I imagined that she might want to apologise, what with her being a grown adult woman now, perhaps she was a mother, perhaps she could see things in a new light, but instead she said: And how about you, what did you end up as?

A lawyer, I said.

Of course, Iris said. You always did have your head in a book. So, are you in the courtroom much, or is it one of those boring office jobs?

A boring office job, I said.

She looked around then leaned in. The corners of her mouth were two sharp points, and her top lip stuck out and up in such a way that her front teeth were visible even when her mouth was closed. I'd always felt that it made her look like a big kid, as if she'd sucked a dummy for too long, but other people probably found it erotic.

Funny that I should bump into you, of all people, she said, lowering her voice. I've got a subtle little legal dilemma on my hands, as it happens.

What Iris Vilden referred to as a *subtle* legal dilemma – I was sure she meant 'sensitive' – was no dilemma at all; a dilemma suggests the need to choose between two unpleasant options. What Iris Vilden actually wanted was for me to help her benefit from a greater proportion of her production's profits.

The distribution of profits between Iris and the writer of her show was all wrong, she told me, she had written large sections of the play herself, not to mention the fact that she'd made use of material from her own life, all of which added up to her being responsible for at least a third of the writing, by her estimate. In spite of this, she said, the writer had run off with all the money.

This isn't really my area of expertise, I told her, and my response caused her brow to arch dangerously.

It had always been difficult to say no to her, even when we were young. I'm not sure whether that said more about me than it did about her, whether she was particularly persuasive or I was easily persuaded.

But, in general... I went on quickly, and her expression softened.

Even though this was clearly an agreement she must have entered into long before the show opened, a fact I couldn't help but point out, I advised her to ask for a meeting with management. I listed three or four arguments she could use in that meeting.

She repeated the points aloud, word for word, asked me to go over them at least seven times, which served only to remind me just how stupid she'd always been at school. Nevertheless, she had somehow landed on her feet – in a career that required her to memorise scripts by heart. She had landed on her feet in the same way she'd always done, I imagined: by making herself irresistibly helpless around men.

As soon as she had a handle on the arguments I'd presented, she thanked me briskly and bid us goodnight before returning to her loosely formed company, who were still busy applauding and laughing.

Nothing had changed, in spite of the fact that I was now a forty-one-year-old lawyer and married mother of two in possession of my own home on the edge of the forest. In spite of all of this, she had me in an iron grip.

I dragged Kai through the pub and let out a heavy sigh when we finally found ourselves back outside.

Why did you want me to *hide* you? Kai asked in bewilderment, and I shook my head.

I was quiet on the way home. He tried asking me what it was all about, but I just stared out of the window.

Was she a childhood friend? he asked, making another attempt to engage me on the subject as we made our way out of Vestli Station and embarked upon the twelve-minute walk home. It was a bright summer evening, but it was chilly. I wasn't dressed for the temperature, and he wrapped his jacket around me before I had a chance to respond to his question.

Iris Vilden had moved into the area and started at our school in year four, seamlessly and harmoniously embarking upon a life that became a daily remake of *Lord of the Flies*. She was blessed with a phenomenal talent for manipulation and for restructuring social constellations. She reigned over us like a one-woman swarm of grasshoppers, razing friendship after friendship to the ground, freezing people out, spreading rumours and then making peace again in a monstrously finely-tuned come-in-from-the-cold routine.

You never knew which day it was: would it be your turn to experience humiliating loneliness during breaktime, or someone else's time to be put through the mill?

The intense relief and delight we felt at being included in the muted warmth that young Iris Vilden seemed to emanate left us powerless to coordinate any form of protest, we were helpless to resist. There was something weirdly democratic about it all too, she was our elected leader.

What I remember most clearly was the unadulterated joy we felt when we found ourselves in Iris's sights. But she didn't carry on the way she did because she was having a hard time at home or struggling with her self-image, it wasn't a symptom of something else, as I tend to tell the boys whenever they witness someone being unkind: they're just sad about something, I say. No. She delighted in what she did, pure and simple.

Then one day, one otherwise normal day in year six, everything changed; I had a divine moment of clarity and realised that I didn't actually *need* to be part of her court. It was that simple. It took only a split second for Iris to lose the power she held over me. On my way out of the classroom, I slipped away from her and attached myself to the small sub-category of girls in our class that lacked any real street cred, an innocent, less well-proportioned group of individuals.

There turned out to be a glorious sense of freedom in that resignation. A much more comfortable existence that I enjoyed well into high school, even though I was still in Iris's class there too.

During my time at high school, my father, a cautious and precise man, was the deputy head teacher. This had very little real impact on my life until one spring day in year nine, when he stepped in as our substitute teacher for maths.

Towards the end of the lesson, as he made his way around the classroom to help each of us with our work in his own gentle way, a commotion broke out at the back. It was Iris making a racket, and I turned around to see my father draw back with a look of terror on his face, as if he'd been burned, as Iris shouted, *Don't touch me!* Then looked up at the class: *He touched me!* She stood up and stormed out, swiftly followed by her two most loyal supporters.

She sat on the stairs during break and wept as the two girls comforted her; a breaktime supervisor came over to speak to her and the news spread through the school like wildfire.

And even though I knew my father hadn't touched her, I was annoyed at him, I wouldn't be seen in public with him for as long as the rumours continued to swirl around, he had been branded. A contempt for him began to grow within me, not because I believed that he'd done anything he shouldn't have, but because he'd been stupid enough to put himself in a position where he too could fall victim to Iris's ways, such a long time after I'd assured myself that I was untouchable.

Wow, Kai said, stopping in the middle of the flight of stairs. I didn't know that.

No, why would you? I replied.

You could have said something…

Now do you understand why she's the reason I have an involuntary, inbuilt scepticism towards any woman who drags a MeToo story out into the open? I said.

Well, if it's been twenty-five years since you saw her last, it might be another twenty-five before you see her again, Kai said, opening the door.

But that wasn't to be.

The following week, an unknown number tried getting through to me when I was at work, and because I was expecting a call from a colleague, I picked up the phone.

She was effusive. She had just come out of a successful meeting at the theatre, she and the writer were to have an equal share of the profits.

Equal? I said, the word slipped out before I could stop it, how did you manage that?

But she ignored my question, and I knew the answer. The writer had realised that this was simply a case of stumping up the money to extricate himself from the situation, anything that would allow him to flee the hive of this queen bee before things grew even more complicated.

I don't know how to thank you, Iris said, and before I had the chance to insist that there was no need, that I was just happy to have been of help, she shouted, Wait! I've got it. And it crossed my mind that I'd just do the easy thing and accept the tickets to her performance, I could always give them to the neighbours, after all.

Thank you, I'd love that – I turned these words over in my mind, focused on how I could make them sound spontaneous, but I didn't have the chance to say them out loud. Instead, Iris suggested that I stay in her holiday home for a week, a cabin by the coast. She hushed me before I had any chance to object.

You simply must, she said. It's glorious out there, I won't take no for an answer!

But I said it all the same. I admitted that the week she'd suggested, the last in June, was indeed my first week of the summer holiday, but that the boys would be away, then I lied and told her that Kai had to work.

What does he do? she asked me without pause.

I wanted to tell her that he was a diplomat or a surgeon, but I told her the truth, that he was a joiner.

She was silent for a moment, then said: That's *very* interesting, Karin.

She asked for my email address. I gave her my private address rather than my work one, refused to give her the satisfaction of knowing that I was an unassuming civil servant when she might otherwise believe that I worked in a government department of note. It didn't take long for her to send through the plans for a jetty she wanted to have constructed by her cabin.

I showed the plans to Kai.

What's all this, are you my agent now? Kai asked, before studying the plans.

After eating, Kai started carrying tools and materials down to the old jetty, which had to be deconstructed and removed before he could start work on the new one, while I sat with my back to the wall of the cabin, along with a beer and a novel I'd borrowed from the library. The hot midday sun burned my face; I was out of the wind from this angle.

I read one page before reaching for my phone and searching 'Iris Vilden + cabin'.

A short interview with Iris popped up, a summer piece from last year, where she mentioned how her boys, aged four and six, would collect mussels – my own boys, aged seven and nine, were still scared of crabs and seaweed – which they would steam over a fire by the water's edge, while their father, Mikkel Wexøe, cooked pasta in seawater. Iris didn't perform any duties herself, it would seem.

This was truly a slice of paradise for her family. It came as no surprise to discover that the cabin had been designed by the high-end architectural firm Snøhetta, and the thought of what it must have cost made my head spin. And all this on Iris's unreliable actor's salary?

Pandora's box had been well and truly opened. I typed

Mikkel Wexøe's name into the search engine, I couldn't help myself, I was so curious to know where the money had come from. I came across several results from the business pages of various newspapers and clicked without hesitation, devouring one article after the next while simultaneously regretting embarking upon my search in the first place.

Back in the early 2000s, Mikkel Wexøe had set up a company manufacturing solar panels, and things had been on the up for him since. Nowadays he was involved in hydrogen and property.

I groaned inwardly, realised that I wanted to know as little as possible about this Croesus made rich by renewable energy. I put down my phone, sipped my cold beer straight from the can and quickly grabbed my phone once again. I simply couldn't help myself; I was drawn to Iris Vilden's family life like a moth to a flame.

There were very few results when I ran an image search, just paparazzi-style pictures of him on his way in and out of cars wearing dark suits and with his hair slicked back. He had clearly adopted the classic role of a media-shy millionaire, constructing a myth about his own mysterious nature, then upholding it.

Mikkel Wexøe's pet project, as I learned upon further reading, was some sort of search engine he had developed for potential property buyers.

My jaw dropped as I read. The more I learned, the more I felt I was plumbing new depths. If you were to type an address into Mikkel Wexøe's property search engine – of an apartment or house you were thinking of viewing, for instance – you would immediately have access to an enormous volume of information about that particular property: private information about the seller, including their annual income, profession and educational qualifications, as well as the details of any properties they'd owned previously. The profession, educational qualifications and annual salary of any potential spouses were also included, and the same was true for any children the seller might have.

More than this, though: you would have access to information pertaining to any neighbours within a radius of your choosing. Salaries, professions, nationalities. Political leanings, religious affiliations, previous convictions, plus links to any social-media profiles they might have.

The average grades and results of any national examinations in all schools within the catchment area. The ethnic composition of each individual class at each individual school and nursery in the area. A pie chart showing annual salaries within the neighbourhood, all handily compiled in one diagram. And all of this within a radius of your choosing! The distribution of professional sectors within the area. School performance and higher-educational choices of the local children and young people.

A socioeconomic survey. Nothing about how old the pipework in the property might be, nothing about damp or dry rot or central heating. Only the success rate of each neighbourhood judged within the narrow framework of income and education.

An instrument of segregation for upper-middle-class people looking to move house, for those who aspired to move up in the world, to lump themselves together in ethnically Norwegian enclaves of culture, media, academia, politics and trade.

It was all completely above-board, publicly available information. Mikkel Wexøe had simply developed what I assumed to be an algorithm that automatically gathered and processed all of this into one enormous database accessible upon payment of a one-off sum.

I stood up impulsively as loud crashes from Kai's tearing apart of the old jetty cut through the silence.

I pictured the family portrait on the wall inside. The soulless businessman with his cold stare, a shell of a man married to a twerp of an actress, father to two little lords with an inherent sense of entitlement, from the day they were born fed with the idea that weakness warranted contempt.

All of a sudden I was overwhelmed with a feeling that I couldn't get away fast enough, and I stomped down the cement steps – cement paid for in blood, I thought to myself, but blood was an exaggeration, more like cement paid for by people's inherent fear of being anywhere near anyone different to them, fear of ending up snared in a maelstrom of socioeconomic poverty – furious that Iris Vilden had somehow managed to make it seem like a grand act of generosity to allow us poor, unfortunate folks to stay here for the week – a *week*, what on earth were we going to do for a whole week? – and I was all the more irritated when I realised that the steps didn't end on land like any normal steps would, but instead led down into the sea, the flight of steps ended underwater! – to where Kai stood sweating with a crowbar in his hand. He stopped and looked at me.

Did they dam up the entire Skagerrak strait just to build these silly bloody steps? I shouted, and Kai gazed at me inquisitively.

What's up with you? he asked.

Nothing, I said, because I couldn't win, not against the kind of people who flouted the laws of nature to construct a flight of stairs, and with my eyes on the gleaming white boats zipping back and forth in this summertime paradise, I tried to regain control, to shake off Iris and the jackal she was married to. Why should I give them any power over me?

Why should I so much as *think* about them when it's the last thing I want?

I can render them insignificant with the power of my mind, I thought to myself. I've done it before. Completely and utterly insignificant.

After breakfast the following day, having pulled on my trainers and stepped out onto the smooth, grey coastal rocks with their stripes of pink, I pondered the reactions that had been awakened deep within me by this recent, involuntary contact with Iris Vilden and/or this insight into her life.

Not envy, I thought to myself, I felt absolutely no envy whatsoever. I didn't want to know anything about them, not really, not about their lives, not about the industries they worked in or the business models they ascribed to, and definitely not about who they associated with, which restaurants they liked, who visited them out here, who slept in their four spacious guest rooms or who used the two guest bathrooms.

The dissatisfaction that comes from comparing myself with others was more my cup of tea. Relative deprivation – having very little while living among others with a great deal. I was constantly on the lookout for it, it was something of a proactive relationship, in truth. Fifteen years ago, I'd decided never to engage with social media to prevent it playing havoc with my psyche. But even so, it was always there.

I had slept badly; I hadn't been able to shake the thought

of all the nights Iris and Mikkel Wexøe had lain there in bedsheets as white as the driven snow, brushed cotton, a different world altogether from our crepe bedsheets back at home. The duvet was thick and stiff, it felt heavy yet soft. And even the loo roll was soft and thick.

I waved at Kai down below, who had now dismantled the old jetty. He was on his knees with a drill in one hand, screwing together new joists, he nodded in my direction.

More than anything, I wanted to see Mikkel Wexøe languish in prison for his quasi-fascistic search engine. Imagine starting off with solar panels and ending up pushing segregation.

As I walked in the sunshine, I tried once again to shake it off, I was on holiday, I told myself, just on holiday, and a free holiday at that, amazing... That was Kai's uncomplicated approach to the matter, and now it was mine too.

I walked what must have been north along the coastline, there were smooth rocks as far as the eye could see, interspersed with the odd sad-looking pine tree, and I was genuinely curious about how far away the nearest neighbour might be. Had Mikkel Wexøe bought up the entire area? I was sure I'd seen a whole row of rooftops when I checked the map on my phone, but the distances had to be greater than they'd appeared on the map.

I thought about making my way around the peninsula,

but there were deep chasms in the rock where the waves crashed in, filling them with water, and in other spots I found myself suddenly on a rocky precipice, forced to turn away from the water's edge and back inland. Rocks always appeared so easily traversable in satellite images, but the reality was very different.

I clambered up a slope, green vegetation clinging to the hillside, wiry, yellow clumps of grass and windswept mini pine trees, then hauled myself up with the help of slender branches that felt as if they'd give way at any moment.

When I eventually climbed back onto my feet and looked around me, I found that I was up by the cabins I'd seen on the map. They basked in the warmth of the sun, lined up along the west coast. I had assumed that the location of Iris's cabin had been selected for its secluded majesty, nestled in a special spot of its own, but perhaps the site they'd ended up in was simply beneath the dignity of other wealthy folks?

Feeling slightly ashamed at how pleased this new insight made me feel, yet uplifted by my discovery all the same, I followed a trail – the pathways crisscrossed here, the unassuming vegetation well trodden by earnest, well-to-do ramblers – and I made my way down a gentle, green section of meadowland as a mild breeze tickled my face, towards the much more human side of the headland, and after a while arrived back down by the water with a never-ending view of the rocky shoreline.

I followed the water's edge, rounded a small peninsula and instinctively jumped, stopped in my tracks by the sudden sight of a man standing just fifteen metres away from me. He was out on a small rock, gently swinging a fishing rod back and forth. I'd grown so used to being on my own, it was like he'd come out of the blue. I carried on walking. He must have caught sight of me out of the corner of his eye, because he stopped swinging his rod for a moment and turned his head just far enough to register my presence before turning back to the water once again.

My instinct was to leave, to vanish, but that would have been odd, so I kept going, onwards over the rocks in the same direction, in his direction.

He had suntanned, hairy legs and was wearing washed-out red shorts, they were almost pink in colour. A grey T-shirt and a rather weather-beaten face framed by loose, dark-greyish locks of hair. He stood there, motionless except for the swinging of his rod, aware that I was approaching without once looking in my direction.

I clambered around yet another rock, and now the horizon opened up before me and I realised that the man wasn't standing on a rock, but on a small stone jetty. An ochre-coloured, old-fashioned-looking cabin appeared behind him, it looked to have been built in the fifties, white door frames, a green lawn, white garden furniture in the shade of an enormous tree, an outhouse the same colour as the cabin, a tiny kingdom, and I stopped once again.

Private property, the man said, plain and simple, just like that, the words seemed to escape out of the corner of his mouth.

Sorry? I said. I blurted it out, even though I'd heard exactly what he'd said.

Private property, he repeated, more clearly this time, sounding annoyed, and every fibre of my being longed to make itself submissive in apology, to turn and disappear, but at the same time, what sort of way was that to treat a person, a fellow human being, a fellow creature of the same species in the same country on the same patch of rock?

Your closest neighbour in a north-easterly direction, treated like unwelcome biomass for disposal? And instead of creeping away, embarrassed and dejected, I drew breath and heard myself speak up, shrewd and on form:

Now then, have you caught anything decent?

He reeled in, moving quickly, yanking the bait out of the water, vexed that I hadn't acted accordingly after he'd made it very clear that I should turn around and disappear, but still refusing to meet my gaze.

The water's swarming with fish down by us, I said,

sounding calm, cool and collected. Shoal upon shoal of mackerel.

'Down by us', I'd phrased it that way on purpose, so he'd know that I wasn't some random pauper sneaking around, fishing out of *necessity*.

He half turned and squinted at me.

You'll have to let me know if you find yourself going without, I said, with a flicker of a smile. We've got plenty to go round.

Then I turned around and walked back the way I'd come. For my return journey, I found a far more efficient route, straight over the headland rather than down by the water, and as I walked through the bone-dry heather and sea thrift, I thought about his face.

I'd seen it before.

Rather than feeling dejected at having been treated like rubbish for collection by our neighbour, I was weirdly fired up. The spontaneous elegance I'd shown when deflecting his comments – so forthright and dynamic, and delivered with such sparkle – had highlighted his miserly dismissal of a woman he didn't know, and was a stark contrast to my optimistic, liberal view of humanity.

Just as I made it to the top of the last hill before reaching our cabin, I caught sight of Kai, who was sweating over his work down by the water's edge, and it occurred to me who the man with the fishing rod was.

It was Per Sinding. The author. Though he was most famously and unavoidably known for being the spouse of another author, the eminent Hilma Ekhult, whose renown completely eclipsed his.

They were so famous that they didn't even live in Norway. Nor did they live in New York, for that matter, which would have made them seem a bit comical or pathetic, really, a poor imitation of Siri Hustvedt and Paul Auster. They were too big for Norway but too small for New York. No, I was sure they lived in Stockholm, which was statement enough in itself: Norway? No thanks. But its closest neighbour? Sure!

Per Sinding had been indignant. Indignant at the fact that an ordinary woman had dared set foot on his private property, or his wife's, as the case may be, since I was fairly certain that of the two of them, she was the only one who actually earned a crust. Per Sinding lived off her the way a chaga mushroom lives off a birch tree. It was thanks to her that he could afford to write his own navel-gazing novels and stand around fishing – fishing with the same fruitless results he saw from his writing, and yet still he felt that he had the right to turn others away with two simple words, 'private property', both of which he'd scarcely bothered to articulate properly.

This was the 'great humanist' Per Sinding, I'd read several interviews he'd given where he came out with cryptic statements about his books, work that didn't seem as difficult to understand as he liked to make out – examples of bitter, self-obsessed autofiction focused on the conflict on his mother's side of the family, ruminations on bad decisions he'd made in the past and obligatory reflections on his own identity, all interspersed with ponderings over the problematic role of men in society.

He was always photographed with the same calculated expression on his face, solemn and stern, his eyes slightly screwed up and surrounded by deep wrinkles, preferably posing under a tree, burdened by no end of pain.

In addition to his narcissistic interviews, he specialised in pompous sermons delivered via op-eds whenever a new crisis arose, preferably humanitarian in nature – he'd refer to his own humanity with passionate zeal, pointing a finger that trembled with rage not only at our elected representatives, but also, rather tactlessly, at all of us.

And yet, he couldn't bear … I started thinking, then realised that my thoughts about Per Sinding were going round in circles, I needed to pull myself out of this spiral, to rise above it.

I shouted down to Kai, who waved back at me, then made my way inside and grabbed the iPad, which was lying on the intimidatingly vast kitchen worktop; I sank down in a chair by the dining table, and this time around I searched 'Hilma Ekhult + cabin'.

In-depth interviews in holiday homes were clearly a genre of their own. I found no fewer than three extensive interviews with Hilma Ekhult, all conducted in her cabin in late summer, and all in connection with a new book, so sheer self-promotion, really, I thought to myself, letting out a little snort as I skimmed the sections outlining the serious themes in her upcoming novel, combined with animated depictions of nostalgic childhood summers spent in this very spot, a never-ending omnibus of small-screen nostalgia, a *Fanny and Alexander* summer special, a big, blurred family in technicolour.

Per Sinding's specialty was bouillabaisse prepared with his own catch, I read, he would serve it up for all the eminent guests who brought their boats up alongside the jetty during the summer months. I could picture them now. Men in pale linen suits with well-trimmed goatees and monocles, members of the Swedish Academy and renowned psychoanalysts, women tottering onto land in high heels, wearing hats that resembled fruit bowls.

I couldn't say that Hilma Ekhult came across as particularly exceptional in any of the three interviews I read. She was too measured, everything was too orchestrated, from the delectable pie made with homegrown berries and the freshly brewed coffee in the daintiest of old-fashioned porcelain cups to the ice-cold elderflower cordial and the comments she made, everything was too well thought-out, she didn't slip up even once; Hilma Ekhult was astute and highly knowledgeable in her interviews and her writing, she quoted great thinkers from east and west alike without difficulty – though never any Norwegians, that would be too trifling and provincial.

Even in her depictions of seemingly carefree summers at the cabin, which had been in Hilma Ekhult's family for as long as the antique coffee pot and porcelain cups, she said – she made it sound as if it was a case of several centuries, rather than decades – she was very careful to highlight the fact that her memories were distinct from other ordinary people's happy memories of summer days by the sea.

Briefly, and laden with insinuation, she spoke about the anxiety she'd always felt when it came to what she called 'the depths', feeding her interviewers tiny drips of information about how she would lie on her stomach on the jetty as a child and stare into the dark water, captivated, while all around her she heard the sounds of laughter and play, she talked about the pull she had felt, as if she were being enticed downwards, as if these depths she spoke of threatened to swallow her whole. Hilma Ekhult doled out these titbits of information in all three interviews to make very clear that she had been a unique child.

The most recent interview was seven years old. Hilma Ekhult hadn't published a novel or given any further interviews in the years since then, as far as I could make out. I read the articles with a stern expression on my face, grunting every time she said something 'wise', yet also well aware that it wasn't a dislike for Hilma Ekhult that was to blame, but an underlying sense of indignation at having been well and truly dismissed by Per Sinding.

In truth, Hilma Ekhult was one of my favourite authors.

I had read everything she'd ever written. Her novels had moved me deeply when I was in my twenties; back then, I'd read with an openness to anything and everything that seemed existentially relevant, as one does at that age.

But Hilma Ekhult was the real deal, she wrote with a sense of urgency, or at least that was my take at the time, and I'd felt the same in my thirties when a further two novels were published. She was absolutely the real deal, which was why it was so surprising when she married Per Sinding.

But wasn't that the case when it came to almost all artists? One always had an authenticity the other lacked. And oddly enough, in most of these cases, it was the woman who was authentic and the man who was found wanting, the woman was sincere and the man was a show-off. Both suffered in their own ways, but one suffered for real and the other for pretend, as my boys used to say back in their pre-school days, and as I still tended to say, uncertain whether it was a childlike way of putting it or not.

Hilma Ekhult wrote Ibsen-esque modern tragedies reminiscent of chamber plays. They were accessible and intellectual all at once. The key to Hilma Ekhult's success, in my eyes at least, was that she pandered to the sophisticated frontal lobe through her thoroughly considered, cool linguistic choices and her precise, restrained depictions, all while her intricately forged plots set among the upper echelons of society – her protagonists tended to be art gallery CEOs, heads of departments, successful architects and the like – and revelations from the past appealed to the more primitive parts of our brains, those that revelled in gossip and sex and self-assertion.

Her novels had been reviewed in the *New Yorker*, and she was the only Norwegian author to be interviewed in depth by the *Paris Review*.

But now she was here.

I opened the map and first checked out my own cabin from above, the grey rooftop that looked like two rectangles that had collided at a 120-degree angle, the patio, the old jetty down by the almost-white rock, and the sea beyond that, turquoise at first, then suddenly almost black.

Then I followed the path I'd tried taking, along by the water initially, then zigzagging until Hilma Ekhult's cabin came into view beyond a headland, located in a snug little bay of its own. Considerably smaller than the cabin I was sitting in, but with a great deal more soul, and more foliage too; I'd caught a glimpse of a small row of deciduous trees towards the back of the property that cast a pleasant shade.

I zoomed in close. A row of small benches and chairs came into view, arranged around what could be a stone table, there were places to sit everywhere you looked, meaning she and Per could move around to suit themselves whatever the weather, there would always be a shady spot, even in the middle of the day in the height of summer.

There was a green lawn in front of the cabin, with a long table in the shade of a large tree, and then the lawn turned into sandy beach, completely white, followed by turquoise shallows and a diving board a little further away on a rock, like something from a different era.

I imagined Hilma Ekhult sitting on the beach in her enormous, wide-brimmed sun hat and a maxi dress made of lightweight, luxury fabric, sitting there reading the work of her favourite Western thinkers, making notes in the margins and taking the odd sip of something or other, I don't know, a mimosa, maybe? And all while Per Sinding was knee-deep in the sea, his legs brown, gathering shellfish for that evening's pasta vongole. And here I was, wearing my shoes indoors, sucked into squinting at the map on my iPad, my only source of insight into their lives.

I imagined evenings around that table, the trees filled with lights and flickering candles everywhere. Late dinners paired with expensive wines, refined conversation with charming guests: theatre directors, publishers, art collectors, patrons of the arts and members of the royal family, if that wasn't taking things a step too far, and in this imagined version of events I realised that I assumed Hilma Ekhult and her husband chose not to mix with any of their actual colleagues – their fellow authors or artists – I couldn't help it, I simply couldn't picture Hilma Ekhult showing any interest in conversations with her peers, but instead imagined her aspiring to a level above that, mingling with those who made – and lost – money from those working in the arts, the administrative premier league, those who knew their Bourdieu from their de Beauvoir, but who could also wrap their heads around a budget.

I felt dirty. Dirty from standing there, scratching at the door of a stranger, yearning to get in, just to *see*, not to partake, but to see, to observe their lives.

But I had something, too. I had a family. A kind husband and two children who were all doing well. A house in dire need of renovation – that was the downside of being married to a joiner, our own house was always last on the list – located in a family-friendly neighbourhood just by the forest, and all within walking distance of anything you might need, and a short half-hour by car or public transport to the city centre.

I had a stable job that I was good at, and I was always very careful to avoid any conflicts that might crop up at work.

I allowed my gaze to follow my return route to my own cabin, up over the hillside rather than via the impassable detour along the water's edge, it was possible to make out a path that split away, a greyish pathway over the dry yellowish-green hillside, and I pictured the person who had recently wandered there, relatively nimble on her feet, content at having successfully mobilised some form of resistance to the humanist Per Sinding's attempts to dehumanise her.

Kai was kneeling on the jetty in nothing but his shorts, screwing in one plank after another. It was hot, even with the slight breeze. I was certain he hadn't applied any suncream, he just sat there and burned in the sun.

Shall we take the boat out? I suggested, and he glanced up at me in surprise.

On the way out, my gaze fixed on the cabin as it grew smaller and smaller, I thought about how strange it was that Iris, who was married to a millionaire, had nonetheless asked *me* for help when it came to pocketing an additional few thousand kroner for herself, and all at the expense of a writer who wasn't particularly well paid. There was no doubting the fact that Mikkel Wexøe was well acquainted with a whole host of lawyers; he might even have had a whole legal department at his beck and call. And yet of all those people, it was me sitting here in this cabin bought with blood money, on day two out of seven.

It was as if she'd wanted to involve me in the shameful exploitation of a vulnerable profession from the moment she'd caught sight of me in the pub that evening.

I asked Kai to take the boat around the headland that I'd

stumbled and fumbled my way around earlier that day. I was wearing sunglasses and felt a flutter in my stomach as we chugged around the point and the next bay came into view. We were sufficiently far away from the shore that I felt no concern that Per Sinding might recognise me as we sailed past, and so what if he did, I thought to myself, I'm his neighbour, we've got every right to be here. But even so, I had made sure to change my outfit before we'd set off.

As we chugged along on the water, Per Sinding was nowhere to be seen. There was only the ochre cabin, way inland.

This cabin had also been cleverly positioned within the surrounding landscape. It was low and partly concealed by pine trees and rocks, but from one particular point out at sea the entire cabin came into view, all of it, right there, the flagpole with its pennant, the rock with its diving board at the far end of the tiny white beach, even the long table on the flat lawn. It was like the most perfect illustration from the most perfect children's book.

I bristled at the thought of Mikkel Wexøe selecting that particular windswept hillside to build his cabin on. Why? Why not a cosy bay like this one? Was it more important to *own* such a place than it was to actually spend any time there? I suspected that to be the case, as I sat there like a spy with a little too much interest in prying, my face angled slightly away, my eyes locked on Hilma Ekhult's tiny paradise from behind my dark sunglasses.

There wasn't a soul to be seen. The boat was by the jetty. There would be no risk of us bumping into them out here, at any rate. They were probably sitting at one of their elitist stone tables drinking sour elderflower cordial.

I realised that it bothered me deep down, the idea that this famous pair of authors was so close by, and I felt a sense of dread when I imagined that they might have returned to Stockholm, or when I considered that Hilma Ekhult herself might never have been here at all.

I wanted to share all this with Kai, yet simultaneously I didn't, he wouldn't get it. He wouldn't understand why I felt so elated to have discovered who owned the cabin along from ours, I didn't understand it myself. At the same time, it was wrong not to tell him about it, that would mean I was keeping it a secret, and why would I do that? *Do you know who owns that cabin?* I opened my mouth to ask, but Kai beat me to it, suggesting we take the boat into town and pick up some prawns.

We paired the prawns with ice-cold German wheat beer, which Kai and I both preferred to white wine. Kai sat in the shade, his shoulders and forehead and nose a shade of deep red bordering on purple. I sat in the sun, which was in the process of setting over the mountain. I glanced at the clock.

But... I said.

Hmm? Kai said.

It's only half-seven.

And? he said.

They barely get any sun here at all! I said.

True, but the light in the morning is incredible – why are you laughing?

I felt a ripple of warmth move through my chest and stomach, took a deep breath. Windswept and shady. Iris's cabin. Wasn't she mortified by the whole thing?

It's still sunny down by the jetty, if you want us to move, Kai said. It'll set before too long.

No, no, I said. This is perfect.

I had called the boys. It was virtually impossible to get them to answer any of my questions, to tell me anything at all, my in-laws would let them sit in front of the television and fiddle with the remote control to their hearts' content during our phone calls.

Afterwards I was overcome with the sense that I was gradually, inevitably, losing them to society at large.

When they were younger, I held them in the palm of my hand. I could imprint my preferences upon them, within reason, my taste in music, the food I liked to eat, but nowadays I could only stand by and watch as everything I'd nourished them with was driven out in favour of tastes imposed upon them by group dynamics.

All the stories I'd told them. Every Greek myth I could get my hands on. It had started with the minotaur, who they had loved, then I'd regaled them with the rest of the tales of Theseus by memory, including the dumping of Ariadne for Phaedra, which had left them both thoroughly stunned.

Then we had ploughed our way through whatever mythology we could get our hands on at the library, though I'd done my best to weed out the worst of the cannibalism and incest.

When we'd made our way through everything the library had to offer, I'd eventually perched myself on the edge of the bed with my phone in my hand and read the Wikipedia entries for the tragedies of Euripides and Sophocles.

They had lain there in their beds, both listening keenly, eyes like saucers.

They're going to be professors of cultural history! I'd thought to myself naively, though now, just two short years later, it was all gone in favour of braindead kiddie culture with no real heart.

Don't call them when they're watching TV next time, Kai said, unflustered even after all my complaints, call them after breakfast instead.

I told Kai that I'd googled who owned the cabin. Mikkel Wexøe. I told him where the money came from, about the fascistic search engine. Kai barely raised an eyebrow.

Golden ghettos, he said, shaking his head. I've seen a few of those in my time.

He's trying to build himself up into some sort of media-shy finance mogul, like that market trader who lost everything, you know the one.

Einar Aas, Kai said. I restored an old boathouse on his neighbour's land.

But can you imagine it? I said, all worked up. Can you imagine earning a living in such a way? Endorsing *segregation*?

People and property, it's a volatile combination, Kai said. Nothing surprises me these days.

And here's the proof, I said, throwing out an arm. This place doesn't even get any sun in the evenings!

Kai looked at me with surprise.

You don't think you're a tad more preoccupied with her than she is with you, eh? he asked.

That's what's so annoying. I've spent years of my life trying to rid myself of her, but still, *still,* I find myself imagining fictional conversations with her, upsetting scenes that never actually occurred, getting my own back on her *in my mind*. And *even there* she comes out on top! And what am I to her? Nothing but a miniscule blast from the past that she can exploit for her own benefit.

Exploit? She invited you out here, Kai said.

I groaned.

That's only so I can see her incredible cabin and how overwhelmingly successful she is, and check out her family's portrait hanging on the wall.

You've got a family too, Kai said.

You wouldn't believe how she's influenced the way I do things as a mother, I said. You wouldn't believe the ways I've tried to orchestrate the boys' friendships from the get-go, I've done everything I can to keep them away from the worst kinds of kids, the ones who display manipulative characteristics, the ones I could see made our boys feel unsure or submissive.

Exposure to that sort of thing is much better than trying to shield them from it, if you ask me, Kai said.

Sure, letting them fall over and hurt themselves, or cut

themselves with a knife and draw a little blood, I've got nothing against that. But psychological terror? When their delicate brains are still developing? Really? He looked as if he wanted to change the subject, and that aggravated me. He would always go with the flow while I got involved only reluctantly and was always the one to worry, but maybe Kai was right, maybe it *was* best to simply go with the flow, but I couldn't do it, it made me feel physically sick to see my boys struggle in one way or another, my small, defenceless boys.

I'm not cut out to be a mother, I said. I don't have the thick skin required for the job.

Rubbish, Kai said. You're an amazing mother.

And to rub it all in, she's invited me – us – here. To make sure my holiday is spent in the maximum amount of misery, I said, and Kai looked at me in bewilderment.

I know her, I said, looking at him, I know what she's like, I do.

You know what? I won't let her, Kai said, grabbing me by the arms. He looked at me sternly.

We're going to have a lovely time. A whole week. There's your revenge right there. To hell with her.

I stacked the plates, any leftovers, carried everything in on a tray, filled the dishwasher. I washed my hands and felt myself hankering after a strong drink, I wanted some spirits, it didn't really matter what. There had to be some sort of drinks cabinet knocking about here somewhere, surely? I went through every drawer in the nauseatingly painstakingly-designed kitchen and eventually stuck my head out the window to Kai.

You haven't seen some sort of drinks cabinet in this place, have you?

The third drawer from the left, the bottom one, Kai said. You have to press on it with your foot.

I turned back and tried, carefully pushed it in, and the drawer bounced open. It was a little freezer drawer, and inside was a bottle of vodka and some ice cubes.

Whaaat?! I called out to Kai.

I know, right? Kai said. Will you get me one too?

I found a couple of glasses, filled them with ice and vodka, and moved over to the window to see if Kai wanted anything else, but he was no longer alone.

Towering over him was Per Sinding, round sunglasses

perched on his head and his hands plunged deep in the pockets of his washed-out red shorts.

...the west side, around the headland, I heard him say.

I pushed the glass to one side and dashed outside without pausing for breath, rushing to interrupt the conversation before Kai had a chance to reveal that we were no more than guests, contrary to what I'd suggested.

Per Sinding looked up and his expression remained unchanged as I rounded the corner; I smiled as if in disbelief, curious, as if I didn't recognise him straight away.

Sorry, I said. Private property.

It was risky and disarming in equal measure, but Per Sinding opted to handle the situation with a smile. He had a slightly aquiline nose, I could see that now, and arrogant flared nostrils that made his smile appear ambiguous, or at least not entirely honest.

Kai gazed at me in disbelief.

We bumped into each other when I was on my walk earlier today, I explained.

It's lovely up here, Per Sinding said, turning to look at the sea. A little exposed to the elements compared to our place...

Kai inhaled, about to explain that we were simply guests here, but I interrupted him.

That was what really drew us to the place, I said, looking

at Kai, holding his gaze. A cabin is the kind of place where you want to feel close to nature, don't you think?

Per Sinding opened his mouth to defend his in-laws' tiny, far more sympathetic, summer kingdom, but I felt certain I could see him beginning to consider his cosy Ekhult paradise as fairly typical, perhaps somewhat banal?

Then it was as if he switched tack mid-flow, decided that attack was the best form of defence, and he said: Nature is best enjoyed from a distance, isn't that what they say? followed by a slight guffaw in Kai's direction.

Kai said nothing, just stared at him and lifted his bottle to his lips, looking a tad haughty.

Per Sinding appeared to be regretting stopping by in the first place. Then it was as if he found fresh ammunition. He sniffed loudly two or three times, like a wolf, then he caught sight of the double-bagged prawn shells by the front door.

Prawns? he said. What happened to all your mackerel?

I glanced quickly at Kai and responded very calmly.

We had them for lunch. The rest are in the freezer.

You freeze your mackerel? Per Sinding said, and he wrinkled his nose ever so slightly.

Of course, I said. You can get a good three months out of them that way.

The response gave us – the owners of an ostentatiously luxury cabin – an unexpectedly flattering and level-headed edge that appealed to me. It didn't expose us; rather, it explained where our wealth had come from.

Well, Per Sinding said, apparently tired of trying to catch us out. I'd best be getting on.

Nice to meet you, Kai said breezily.

Come on over sometime, Per Sinding said. We're here for the week, then it's back home to Stockholm for us.

He dropped in the last part with all the nonchalance he could muster, no doubt hoping to pique our curiosity, or to impress us, at the very least.

We might well do that, Kai said.

We said our farewells, and Per Sinding turned around and eventually disappeared behind the rock, first his brown legs, then his long back and eventually the back of his head and his sunglasses, which flashed in the sunlight.

Now then, Kai said when we were alone once again.

Do you know who that was? I asked him.

No, who?

Hilma Ekhult's husband.

What, the author? Kai said, picking at his teeth.

I bumped into him on my walk. That's why he came, I said. He's walked all the way here just to confirm that the dishevelled woman who got lost and meandered onto his property earlier doesn't actually have a cabin around here after all.

Uh huh, and why exactly did you lie to him?

Didn't you see the way he looked at us? I asked. As if it was beyond all reason that two people like us could own a place like this?

Well, sure, Kai said, and don't you think it *is* beyond all reason?

It was hard to know how to spend my time, surrounded on all sides by wind and water and rock. I refused to take any more walks in the countryside around the cabin. I felt a persistent sense of dread that I might bump into Per Sinding again.

The notion that this magnificent humanist had never even bothered to get to know his own neighbours out here came as no surprise; we'd enjoyed a small victory over him, but it was important that we didn't push the envelope.

All the same, I felt a strange pull westward to their bay, intrigued by the notion that she – Per Sinding had said 'we', after all – was there.

Kai took the odd break from his work and taught me to drive the boat, but we were careful to go in the opposite direction of their cabin. We chugged around various points along the coast and into small inlets, always on the lookout for small, hidden stretches of beach where we could take the boat inland, go for a swim and eat the lunch we'd brought out with us, but there were cabins and other people everywhere.

More often than not, we would stop in the shallows and

fish, not too far away from several other small boats engaged in precisely the same activity. It had a practical function, at the very least. Nothing in this kingdom belonged to us, nothing other than the few pollocks that we managed to fish out of the water.

By the time our fifth day rolled around, the Friday, I'd had so many imagined conversations with Hilma Ekhult that I'd begun to tire of her company.

As a rule, at twilight she and I would sit outdoors at one of the round stone tables with a glass of ice-cold rosé each, and the menfolk, as I called them, would sit down by the water and have a beer, chatting quietly.

During these conversations, I'd articulate ideas about Hilma Ekhult's writing that nobody had ever conveyed with such precision or insight, nobody had ever delved so deeply into the essence of Hilma Ekhult's novels. And Hilma Ekhult herself, who usually felt no need or desire to hear the grovelling interpretations of the art she produced, listened deeply and held my gaze, nodding gravely when I mentioned anything particularly astute, barely able to get enough of what I had to say.

She hadn't had a book published in seven years, and together we did our best to dissect the issues she was so obviously coming up against. I listened patiently and analytically. It was evident that she had reached a point in her career where everything suddenly felt meaningless, she was plagued with doubts about the art she produced because she had misgivings about her own worth as a person, and thanks to my intelligence, Hilma Ekhult found that she not only admired me, but also began to fear me, and it was at this point that our fictional conversations broke down, time after time.

Shall we go home? I asked Kai at breakfast. We were both perched on bar stools at the kitchen island, I was wearing Iris's white bathrobe. I'd been persuaded to take a morning swim, lowering myself into the water from the newly-constructed jetty, and it had been ice-cold at first, then very pleasant, Kai and I had circled one another like two seals. Kai had been delighted to see me in the water, and I had wondered all the while whether it was a genuinely pleasant experience, or if I was simply playing along.

Home? Kai said. Now?

It's going to be heaving around here over the weekend.

Heaving with what?

Rich people, I said.

But I want to stay, Kai said. I'm finally done working. *My* holiday has only just started!

You didn't even want to come at first, and now you don't want to go home, I said irritably.

Didn't want to come? he said, getting up. He popped his coffee cup under the machine nozzle and pressed the button, the buzzing of the coffee grinder drowned out my response.

... just don't want to be here any longer!

Relax a bit, won't you? It's a free holiday, he said, he leaned on the kitchen worktop as the coffee trickled into his cup in two fine streams.

Things are always so uncomplicated for you, I said.

But how complicated can they really be? he asked, placing the cup of coffee down in front of me. The two of us out here alone, no kids to look after. How often does that happen?

He threw his arms around me from behind and kissed my neck. I sighed in response.

Karin, he said sternly. Come on, now.

I don't like it here, I said.

He placed his hands over my ears and turned my head so I was looking out at the panoramic view, the still, blue sea that merged so perfectly with the sky above.

I get it, he said, I mean, just look at that awful view!

He kissed my neck again and I closed my eyes so I would be spared from gazing upon the horizon everyone clearly found so enchanting. I tried picturing something else, anything else, as Kai slipped his hands inside Iris's bathrobe and began touching my breasts, and I sighed again, but now it was more of a moan, and I had to be careful not to fall off the wobbly bar stool.

We'd be better off in bed, I said, slipping down from the stool as he kissed me, and then his phone started vibrating on the kitchen worktop.

Don't... I said, but he glanced at the screen and then at me. I need to take this, he said. Don't go anywhere.

He grabbed his phone and stepped outside, and I stood there for a moment then started to clear the table. I rinsed the dishes under the tap and looked at Kai, who was on the phone outside, and even partly facing away from me I could see that he was smiling, he looked so happy, and I thought to myself: does he ever look that happy when he's with me, or do I weigh him down with my Eeyore-like disposition, do I extinguish any glimmer of joy or ecstasy, does he burn up all his energy trying to perk me up?

I turned around and picked up the cheese and ham, made up my mind to change, but I knew in the same instant that I was doomed to failure.

Now then, where were we? Kai asked, he'd come back in. He stuck his phone in his back pocket and made his way towards me.

Too late, I said, putting the cheese and ham back in the fridge.

Hey, he said, don't...

Can we go home? I repeated, closing the fridge door and looking at him pleadingly.

What's actually bothering you? he asked.

I'm reliving my trauma, I said without a hint of irony.

Is it her again? he asked.

I said nothing.

If this woman hadn't caused you problems in the past, you might never have become a lawyer, Kai said, encouragingly. Nothing can hold you back!

After finishing my third year of high school, I had immediately moved to Oslo with my best friend to study law. Her parents were lawyers, but mine weren't, there was no reason for me to have any interest in the subject, I was simply tagging along for the ride, but I liked it.

We shared a flat on Colletts gate with three others. I had landed on my feet with virtually no opposition, I was living my life in the capital and loving every moment. My studies were going well and I had started to envisage a career for myself in criminal law.

Then, one afternoon in March during the fourth year of my course, I visited a flat near Vestkanttorget to pick up a second-hand brass floor lamp. On my way home, I crossed Arno Bergs plass heading for an alleyway on Gyldenløves gate, pleased with my purchase and skipping along a little too quickly, as I tended to do in parts of town I didn't know too well, and completely inadvertently, I stumbled onto a film set.

Just two metres away from me stood Iris Vilden, leaning against the trunk of a huge, pollarded poplar tree, and across the road was an enormous camera and a group of people standing in a horseshoe; before anybody could cry *cut!*, I did a complete one-eighty, right under her nose, and marched straight out of frame with the same haste I'd marched in, a manoeuvre that must have been bewildering and comical to anyone that happened to witness it. I hurried back onto Schives gate and worked my way home via an enormous loop.

When I got home, I looked up her address in the online directory. She lived two blocks away from me.

I moved out of my flat-share without offering any explanation, bought myself a tiny flat in a nondescript part of Sandaker, and my friend and I gradually drifted apart. I managed to secure a mortgage by working part-time at the off-licence in Sandaker shopping centre for the rest of my studies, and I went on to work there full-time for years afterwards, all while half-heartedly searching for other jobs.

I wouldn't exactly say I have a mental-health problem, but it was a blow, not my brief, idiotic encounter with Iris, she hadn't even seen me, but my reaction to it, it was a symptom, I argued, a manifestation of how little fight was left in me, in spite of all the years I'd had to develop that kind of strength.

This ludicrous solitary existence lasted more than five years and only came to an end when a bearded joiner knocked on my door, a man named Kai with thick, reddish-brown hair. Our apartment management company had made the controversial decision to convert the communal drying loft on the fourth floor into an additional storey for those of us who lived on the third floor, and Kai was the man who would be doing the work.

I don't know how to describe it, other than to say it was like finding a safe haven when all hope seemed lost.

One month later, we were making dinner with the radio on, listening to a couples therapist talking about how important it was never to take your partner for granted.

Kai, who was cutting tomatoes at the time, turned to look at me without pausing his slicing and said: You can take me for granted.

And you can take me for granted, I'd replied.

We took out a huge mortgage one year later, I was pregnant at the time, and bought a house in Skillebekk over in Nittedal. Kai called the house our marriage pact: neither of us could afford to buy the other out if things ever went awry between us. We were comfortably stuck with one another.

I had purposely made an excellent match: while I was insecure and neurotic, Kai was calm and confident. The last thing I needed was someone like me. And the last thing our offspring would ever need would be two of me.

We took the boat out one last time. Kai sat by my side and offered advice as I took the helm, driving slowly, heading south. The sea had never been my thing, never mind sailing on it. It had been one of the most obvious divides when I'd been growing up: those families that had a boat, and those that didn't. I sometimes felt like we lived in two different countries, each with its own language and religion.

I took the job seriously, slowing down whenever any other boats appeared in our path, no matter how far away they were.

Sea as far as the eye can see, I said. Everyone wants a cabin by the sea. But why? What's so great about the sea, can anyone explain it?

You can go fishing, Kai said.

But you can't *drink* it. You can't do anything remotely useful with seawater. It's just daft.

So, you're telling me I can stop saving up for a cabin on the archipelago, then? Kai said.

I just don't understand the appeal, I said. Thousands of people zooming about in boats, pressure to look a certain way, to eat vast amounts of shellfish, and then there's the wind, the seagulls, the never-ending pursuit of prestige. I'd much rather have a little place in the mountains.

I see, so a cabin in the mountains is OK with you, is it? There's no pursuit of prestige involved in that?

Not that kind of cabin, obviously, I'm not talking about some sort of ski resort. Just somewhere simple – a cosy little cabin with a little wood-burning stove. By a small lake.

Uh huh, so you *do* want water, just not saltwater? Leeches and adders are more your thing?

As we made our way around a peninsula not far from the cabin, an old wooden boat appeared ahead of us, a *snekke*, or at least I thought that was what it was called, and chugged in our direction. I slowed down at once, and the other boat did the same, and immediately I spotted who was at what I assumed they called the helm, it was Per Sinding. We approached one another slowly.

And sitting there at the prow, head-to-toe in off-white with a visor on, looking stylish yet somehow also hilarious, like a golfing pensioner from a different era, was Hilma Ekhult.

Per Sinding stopped their motor, and I started to struggle with my steering, it looked as if we were about to bump into each other.

Ahoy there, Per Sinding said, waving at us, and Kai leaned over me and braked hard.

I got to my feet, wobbling as Kai took the helm.

Are you two out voyaging? Per Sinding asked, gliding towards us in the tranquil water.

I tried not to look at Hilma Ekhult in her ankle-length trousers and V-neck jumper and floaty shawl. In the shade offered by the brim of her visor I could just make out a look of indifference, her skin paper-thin and almost entirely wrinkle-free, she was clearly obsessed with protecting herself from the sun. I felt a physical reaction in her presence, a fluttering in my stomach and chest.

Ship ahoy, I said, trying my best to sound relaxed and in control, casually humorous, and Kai flapped a hand to his temple, an ironic greeting, as we passed one another slowly. Hilma Ekhult gave a strained smile in our general direction without making eye contact. It was a great naval battle where showing the least interest in the other party was of highest importance.

It's the neighbours, Per Sinding said.

Oh, Hilma Ekhult replied. Not 'ohh', but 'oh'.

We bobbed up and down in silence, three metres away from one another, the two of them in their charming little *snekke* and us in our streamline, unsympathetic pleasure cruiser, so white and gleaming that the reflected sunlight was blinding.

Out on patrol? Kai said, and I delighted in his nonchalance.

Just out for a breath of fresh air, Per Sinding replied, and I could see that the humidity or the saltwater had given his otherwise loose curls a tighter, more fused appearance.

They might have been ten, fifteen years older than us, at a guess, somewhere in their mid-fifties or thereabouts, while Kai and I were forty-three and forty-one, respectively. They had at least one child, I'd read so much in an interview, they must be almost grown up by now, they studied or maybe lived with them in Stockholm, a half-Swedish child with two fully Norwegian parents, where was the sense in that? If they'd learned German or French or even English, for that matter, any of those would have made some sense, but *Swedish*? And I sensed very clearly that my admiration and reverence for Hilma Ekhult and her work was tainted by a sense of unease now that I'd actually met her in person, perhaps it was some sort of defence mechanism given that she was acting so arrogantly; looking at things objectively, she *was* arrogant.

But she can only look arrogant if I acknowledge her, I thought to myself.

And here we have...? I said, looking cheerfully in Hilma Ekhult's direction.

She gave no indication that she was planning on responding, she didn't even raise an eyebrow beneath her ridiculous visor, but she did allow Per Sinding to act as her spokesperson.

This is Hilma, Per said, and it was obvious that he wished

she didn't have to be introduced as such. Hilma Ekhult, he added, with a glimmer of hope that it might rouse some recognition among us, but Kai and I simply smiled in a friendly manner, giving nothing away.

In her light-khaki outfit, with a visor that might be mistaken for a pith helmet if you weren't looking carefully enough, she reminded me of a colonial overlord crossing a flooded jungle on a river boat. *The horror! The horror!*

And you two are? she asked, surprised, holding my gaze. Her eyes were pale grey in the blazing sunshine, her pupils barely visible.

This is Kai, I said, and he raised a hand affably. And I'm Karin.

Hilma Ekhult smiled, her lips pressed tightly together.

And what was it you said you did, Kai? Per asked.

Me? Kai replied, leaning forward slightly. I felt my eye twitch slightly when he opened his mouth.

I'm retired.

Of course you are, Per Sinding chuckled, and I closed my eyes behind my dark sunglasses. Hilma Ekhult turned her entire body to face Kai, either to weigh him up properly or simply because she had a stiff neck.

Kai looked at them gravely.

I was an energy-market trader for many years, he explained, but I gave that up a while ago.

I expelled all the air from my lungs in one go.

Trading, I see, Per Sinding said eventually. I hear it's like the Wild West.

All perfectly above board, Kai said.

And what's it like in reality? Hilma Ekhult asked, and Kai opened his mouth without saying a word.

It's not that easy to break it down in simple terms, he said eventually.

It's all about predicting changes in price, when it comes down to it, wouldn't you say? I remarked, facing Kai.

And isn't it also true that you can lose everything quite suddenly? Per Sinding asked, a faint flicker of hope in his tone.

Well, not in my case, Kai replied.

Hilma Ekhult turned to face her husband.

Not a world we're acquainted with, she said, her boat bobbing up and down. The seawater reflected the sun and created small waves of light that flickered across her face.

It must have gone well for you, Per Sinding said, given...

He stopped himself, but I knew that he was thinking about our cabin, before realising that acknowledging it was the last thing he wanted to do.

And how about you? he asked me eventually. Are you also retired?

Not quite yet, I said, as I tried to work out my next step.

Kai cast a glance in my direction with a look I interpreted as encouraging.

I suppose you might call me an entrepreneur, I said.

Oh really? Hilma Ekhult replied. She had started to look a little pale, as if she wasn't pale enough already. She must have been hoping that we were merely a couple of blockheads, a hope that was now being squarely quashed.

A female entrepreneur, Per Sinding said, well now, feminism has gone a step too far!

I allowed a terse smile to flicker across my face in response.

So, you manage a small company, do you? he asked eventually.

You could say that, I replied.

In what field? Hilma Ekhult asked.

Property, I replied.

So you're a broker? Per Sinding said.

She was an entrepreneur, she just said so, Hilma Ekhult cut in.

I created a search engine of sorts, I said, taking a breath. For people looking to invest in property.

Then I very casually explained the kind of information my users had access to.

Per Sinding's face darkened, I saw a flicker of abhorrence or condemnation creep over him with every detail that I shared about my socially Darwinistic search engine.

Salary, too? he asked, looking alarmed. Surely that can't be legal?

Salary too. Anything in the public domain. It's just that nobody has compiled it all in one place before now.

Every single address in the country? Hilma Ekhult said, her eyebrow raised.

I confirmed it with a nod, and could see both terror and fascination in her expression.

It's a stretch as far as privacy's concerned, I said, but it's nothing compared to what the tech giants know about each and every one of us.

Doesn't something like this create ghettoes of sorts? Hilma Ekhult asked as she rocked up and down on the bow.

It does, I said, concise and to the point. The wealthy and highly educated have always flocked together. My programme simply streamlines the inevitable, if you like.

Have you no moral scruples whatsoever? she said.

I simply discovered how to earn a living using systems already in place.

I shrugged and flashed them a smile.

It promotes segregation, Hilma Ekhult said. I can't say that I'd be very comfortable with that.

You might be right, I said. But in theory, it can also create diversity. A middle-class couple can use my tool to establish small 'islands' of privilege in less attractive areas, and in the longer term, that can transform entire neighbourhoods.

In theory, Hilma Ekhult said.

For some reason or another, I enjoyed making out that I was an unscrupulous individual with no issue earning a living by making society worse than it already was.

But I sold it, I said. So nowadays I'm just an investor.

Hilma Ekhult let out an apathetic sigh and turned to face her husband in an attempt to encourage him to whisk her away with every haste.

Per Sinding cleared his throat.

We were given some langoustines by a friend today, he said. More than we'll be able to get through ourselves.

Hilma Ekhult looked at him sharply.

I see, I replied neutrally.

So, if the two of you fancied coming over to help us out…? he began, slightly more meekly.

Unfort— I said, but Kai interrupted me.

Shall we come and pick them up now? he asked.

Per Sinding chuckled.

I actually wondered if we might eat together.

We're— I said, but Kai interrupted me again.

Tonight? he asked.

Shall we say late lunch? Per Sinding suggested.

We're off home, actually, I said, looking sternly at Kai.

Sure, but we could do lunch, Kai said. Shall we say five o'clock? And I thought five o'clock, lunch at *five*? but Per Sinding simply nodded his head as he weighed up the suggestion. Lunch at five wasn't an entirely unfamiliar concept to him, what with his continental habits.

That could work, he said eventually, and then the two of them chugged off without a word.

I thought she was your favourite author, Kai said.

But now my favourite author thinks I'm the brains behind a fascist startup! I barked, stomping after him across the smooth coastal rock.

We had decided to delay our departure until early the following day. We'd made sure to eat well before leaving the cabin to prevent us from gorging ourselves on the langoustines, instead planning to pick at them with careful confidence – I'd pulled up a YouTube video where someone demonstrated how to approach such a meal – to make clear that langoustines were nothing out of the ordinary for us.

It was hot, far too hot, we'd have to sit in the shade, preferably down by the water's edge. I'd had some difficulty selecting an outfit, firstly because I hadn't packed much to begin with, and secondly because it was such a hot day; a lightweight dress or pair of shorts would have been the natural choice were it not for the fact that I was reluctant to reveal any more skin than necessary in Hilma Ekhult's company, I didn't want to charge onto her property like some sort of fleshy, sunburned creature without any reservations to speak of.

In the end I had opted for jeans, which was a poor choice, very poor indeed, they clung to the backs of my legs and knees and thighs within moments of pulling them on. My skin and hair, which had momentarily felt clean and dry and freshly washed, was clammy and damp with perspiration.

I had asked Kai to read up on energy trading and economics in case they decided to test his knowledge.

Economics covers a whole host of things, Kai said. I'm a self-employed tradesman. Doesn't that involve a certain degree of economics?

That's *not* economics, I said.

He swaggered along beside me without a care in the world in his blue, nautical-style canvas shorts and a loose-fitting, dove-grey linen shirt. How I envied his working wardrobe as we each went our own way in the mornings – me in my prim attempt at office wear that left me feeling uncomfortable on a daily basis, and Kai, unshaven and wearing baggy trousers covered in pockets, soft wool long johns and thick fleeces and warm scarves and hats in the winter months, and then loose-fitting T-shirts and a cap in the summer to cover his dishevelled hair, paired with long shorts, also covered in pockets.

There was so much that Kai had that I lacked. He compensated for all my weaknesses, offset my inferiority complex with his poised sense of calm. It's not that Kai lacked introspection, but it never sent him into a negative spiral.

I was still angry at him, but at the same time he was right, I had to admit that. Lunch with Hilma Ekhult was a story for the history books, no matter who she thought I was.

We need to carpet bomb them with questions, Kai said, before they have a chance to ask us anything. Per Sinding strikes me as the kind of man who'll be happy enough to talk about himself, at any rate.

We clambered to the top of the final rock and gained a view along the entire west coast, packed as it was with one cabin after the next, and we found that we could see all the way into Hilma Ekhult's cosy, concealed bay, their stretch of coastline, the antiquarian diving board.

They were sitting on the tiny stone jetty, the two of them, both looking relaxed in their chairs – Hilma Ekhult in a black dress and wide-brimmed sunhat, a book in her hands, just as I'd pictured her so many times. Per Sinding was by her side, also with a book in his hands, copious cultural capital on show for all to see.

What made me so sure it was for show, though? Couldn't it simply be an authentic, honest insight into their lives? There they both sat, a pair of artists, each with a book to hand. This was surely a very ordinary scene, the two of them sitting here in such a way.

But no. They knew we were coming, that we'd be with them any second, they *yearned* for us to see them in such a way, to think, oh, *that's* who they are, the sorts with their nose always in a book, with a tinge of envy at their rich inner lives, the crackle and pop of their frontal lobes as they turned page after page, deeply immersed in their reading. They'd spent time orchestrating this, they must have come up with it together – we'll make sure we're sitting here reading when they arrive, OK? – making a show of giving very little thought to their guests, who were due at any moment.

And it disappointed me, when I thought about it, the fact that Hilma Ekhult went along with all of it when it was so clearly the great poseur, Per Sinding, who was behind the whole ruse. She played along against her will, participated in his dreadful performance, when any other reasonable host would be busy pottering around, getting things ready, anxious about the food and table settings and cut flowers, any other two people would be winding each other up about all sorts, haven't you swept the patio yet?!

But no, there was none of that. Two lazy intellectuals, this was the role they had assumed, certain that we would be suitably impressed to see not one but *two* actual books in their hands, curious as to what kind of technology this must be, iPads that *actually* allow you to turn the page?

Hello there! I shouted down to them, a jovial individual in anything but elegant attire, while Hilma Ekhult sat beneath a parasol in her cool, floor-length dress, I wondered which film she was imagining herself to be starring in.

Per Sinding turned his head inquisitively, and on catching sight of us he waved briefly before turning back to his book, giving the impression that he was reading one more sentence before slapping it closed and rising from his chair in an unhurried, calculated manner.

I felt myself beginning to tire of this performance even before we'd really got going, but I decided to rise above it all. To cast the act aside, perhaps even admit that our cabin, which had evidently impressed Per Sinding so much that he'd decided to invite us over for langoustines, actually belonged to someone else: we were nothing but guests and could hardly abide the idea of spending another hour in the place. We'd already packed and were preparing to head home first thing in the morning. Hilma Ekhult could say what she liked.

Per Sinding approached us in an intentionally leisurely manner as we made our way up over the rock, taking care at the steepest points.

He waited at the foot of the rock and extended a gallant hand in my direction; I gripped it tightly as I took my last few steps down.

He was dressed in a loose, white cotton shirt and khaki shorts with sandals. His shirt sleeves were rolled up to reveal two athletic-looking forearms, as if this was a muscle group he'd made a conscious effort to define. You didn't end up with forearms like that from writing, not unless you were attaching some sort of weights to your fingertips.

Welcome to our little patch of paradise, he said, just as I'd imagined he would, and only now did Hilma Ekhult rise from her chair, channelling Mia Farrow, delicate yet strong. She stood motionless by her deckchair for a moment, gazing out at the glittering sea, pensive, or perhaps just casting a critical eye over the scene, before turning and positively *gliding* across the jetty, making straight for us in the long, black, floaty dress that fluttered in the gentle breeze; she moved so slowly, one careful step at a time in her strappy sandals, that the conversation we'd paused while waiting for her had to continue.

A real gem of a place, this, Kai said, taking in the property, from the diving board and the white beach to the stone jetty with its slate flagstones, the natural foliage down by the beach that led up to the cabin, and eventually the cabin itself, all while Hilma Ekhult approached us, one step at a time.

Very nice, I said, and it was clear that Per Sinding wasn't

quite satisfied with our words of praise, he wanted to see us trembling with envy, bowled over by the authentic, pastoral scene before us, such a stark contrast to our cold, soulless cabin that was really better suited to appearing in an architectural biennial than on any actual archipelago.

Shabby chic, isn't that what they say? Kai said, smiling arrogantly, and I felt a deep-seated gratitude to him for finding precisely the right words, somehow both critical and complimentary all at once, while Per Sinding grew doubtful as to how best to respond.

Hilma Ekhult had finally joined us, her attire reminding me of Death in *The Seventh Seal*; she had removed her large sunglasses, which made her look like some sort of grieving widow at a Sicilian mafia funeral when paired with her wide-brimmed hat and black dress.

Her book was tucked under her arm. Ingeborg Bachmann, I read to myself, and inwardly I rolled my eyes, did she really think that Ingeborg Bachmann would impress us, a couple of financiers in their forties with a cabin worth dizzying sums? In the best-case scenario, we'd have assumed her to be some bestselling Swedish crime author or other, we might have looked for her work in the airport bookshop when we took our next business trip.

Welcome, she said formally, with a crackle in her voice that she quickly cleared with a cough.

Thank you, Kai replied politely. It's lovely out here.

She was exquisite. That was the word. Utterly exquisite from top to toe, from the smooth, shiny hair at the nape of her neck that peeped out from beneath her hat when she turned around, to her pale-rose, almost nude-coloured toenail polish in her cognac-coloured leather sandals.

She turned to look at Per Sinding.

Are there to be any refreshments? she asked, her voice deeper now, the skin of her neck taut, delicate-looking.

Of course, refreshments, Per Sinding said, turning on his heel and hurrying off.

So, Hilma Ekhult said slowly after Per Sinding left us, and she turned back to look out at the water. Mostly because she felt uncomfortable at having been left alone with us, I assumed, though it seemed unnecessarily arrogant to simply turn her back on us.

And this place, I said, has it been in the family for long?

In *my* family, yes, she replied bluntly. My grandfather built this cabin with his own two hands. I've spent every summer I can remember here.

Sounds idyllic, Kai said.

To a degree, she said, wasting no time in correcting him, offended that Kai should assume she'd had an uncomplicated childhood.

Per Sinding emerged from the cabin and crossed the

lawn with a jug in one hand and a stack of glasses in the other.

Hilma Ekhult led us from the jetty through a grove of honeysuckle and over to the corner of a low stone wall between the jetty and the lawn. There were cushions on the wall for sitting on. A large, circular stone slab served as a table. The cherry tree behind us cast a pleasant shade over proceedings.

Hilma Ekhult perched her tiny posterior on one of the cushions, while Kai and I positioned ourselves in the little nook opposite. Per Sinding followed with refreshments. He sat down beside his wife and filled all four glasses to the brim.

Cheers, and welcome, Per Sinding said, raising his glass, and we did the same, making sure to lock eyes with everyone present to ward off bad luck before taking our first sip of what turned out to be a slightly-too-strong mojito, as I'd already suspected upon spying the dark-green leaves floundering at the bottom of the jug and thinking to myself: A *mojito*, is that supposed to impress us?

Back when I had been working at the off licence, I had learned that you should never serve spirits as a welcome aperitif, particularly not before serving something subtle in flavour like langoustines – I imagined langoustines to have a subtle flavour, anyway, though I'd never actually sampled them myself – because spirits numb the taste buds. The fact that Per Sinding didn't realise that, what with all his highbrow tastes, left me feeling unexpectedly invigorated.

Lovely, Kai remarked pleasantly.

Hilma Ekhult finally removed her enormous hat, placing it down beside her, and we were actually able to see her head for the first time. Her face was rather small, with delicate features, and her very fair hair was thin, though not tragically so. It was a neat, reserved style.

She exuded an air of discomfort in our presence. This wasn't evident in anything she said, of course, for she said almost nothing at all, but it was obvious in the way that she rarely lifted her gaze, barely even bothering to look in our direction.

And is it you two who own this place, or do you share it with others in the family? Kai asked.

Yes, Hilma Ekhult replied.

Yes to which? I found myself blurting out, sounding unexpectedly harsh yet chirpy, is it just you two, or do you share the place?

Just us, Hilma Ekhult replied.

OK, Kai said, and discreetly rolled his eyes.

Very nice, I said. Less conflict that way.

Ha! Per Sinding chuckled. Any conflict is behind us these days. He took another sip of his drink before raising his glass in our direction.

And so you're a writer? I said, turning to face Hilma.

We're both writers, Per Sinding chipped in hastily.

And what exactly do you write? I asked.

Books, Hilma Ekhult replied.

Why? I asked, the word slipped out before I could stop it.

This simple question left them both perplexed. At first the two of them reacted in precisely the same way, smiling, caught off guard; they looked at one another before Per Sinding locked eyes with me, a moralising air about him.

Why? Well, egoism and aesthetic enthusiasm, he replied. And a sense of historical impulse and political purpose, of course.

I immediately recognised his words, lifted straight from the Orwell essay 'Why I Write'; it was a question that Per Sinding clearly had a habit of googling frequently, given his lack of any actual answer.

I nodded slowly.

Hilma Ekhult had apparently checked out of the conversation altogether; it was all simply too inane for her liking. She sat there with her tiny chin resting on one hand and her legs crossed, unable to fathom why Per Sinding had thought it a good idea to invite us here.

Per grabbed the pitcher, rose halfway from his seat and topped up our glasses, Hilma Ekhult placed a hand over hers to prevent him from doing the same for her.

We toasted once again, our gestures and nods more restrained this time, in truth Per Sinding doing little more than flare one nostril, then we drank in silence, our eyes on the sea.

So, you write about politics? I asked.

Well, everything is political, whether you like it or not, he replied.

Everything? I replied, like some sort of bothersome Socrates, incapable of taking anything at face value. Kai sat there, humming under his breath as he always did when he was thinking about something other than the conversation going on around him.

Per looked to Hilma Ekhult for help.

She raised an eyebrow elegantly, lowered her gaze and cocked her head to one side slightly, with a supercilious, barely there smile that suggested the entire conversation was idiotic simply because Kai and I were part of it.

Every statement we make has a social and political dimension, she concluded curtly.

Of course, I said briskly; of all the paths our conversation might take, I had no wish to end up on this one.

Not *party* political, you understand, Per Sinding stressed.

Hilma Ekhult cleared her throat.

Novels, she said. We write novels.

Oh! I said. How exciting. Crime novels?

God, no, Per Sinding replied, and glanced at Hilma once

again. She had barely touched her drink. I imagined that alcohol might go to a little head like hers quickly in this sort of heat. I could tell by looking at them that our visit would be a short one.

Langoustines, Per Sinding said, getting up quite suddenly. No need for us to hang around, eh?

Do you need any help? Kai asked politely, and he too stood up.

No, no, you sit down, Per said, but Kai followed him nonetheless.

Clearly uncomfortable with the prospect of being left alone with me, Hilma Ekhult stood up too.

We can all go, she mumbled, and so I stood up too.

I picked up the jug, emptied the leaves into the thick tangle of honeysuckle behind the wall and gathered the glasses, a task that Hilma Ekhult realised too late was one she ought to have taken care of.

Let me... she said, offering a hand to take the glasses from me, but I simply smiled and shook my head, I was enjoying playing this disconcerting role, polite and helpful yet morally reprehensible. She picked up her hat and carried that instead.

We walked in a line over the lawn and past the long table under what turned out to be a huge beech tree, all the way over to the cabin door. There were more seats there and, pushed up against the ochre-coloured cabin, a long wooden bench, itself a distressed shade of grey from the wind and weather it had been exposed to.

Kai automatically rapped his knuckles against the wooden cladding.

That needs replacing, he said curtly, and Per Sinding stopped in the doorway inquisitively.

Those two planks of wood there, Kai said, patting them. Rotten.

Per Sinding furrowed his brow.

He's right, Hilma Ekhult said, picking at the woodwork with her index finger. You'll need to see if you can get a hold of the joiner.

I can do that, Kai said, and his seamless shift from trader to tradesman sent an anxious shiver through me.

You must have a few extra planks lying around.

A man of many talents, I see, Per Sinding remarked in a disgruntled tone.

Grew up on a farm, Kai replied. Teaches you most of the skills you need in life.

Per said nothing upon hearing this revelation. He bowed his head and disappeared through the low doorway leading into the cabin.

In the outhouse, Hilma Ekhult said. There's a stack of planks in there.

I followed Per up the steps with the jug and glasses in my hands and followed him into the old-fashioned, pale-green 1950s kitchen.

And what about you? I asked. You must have plenty of those welcome advantages of wealth they talk about these days.

He stopped and turned around upon catching the literary reference I had unwittingly alluded to.

You must be the first greedy capitalist I've met who's read the Mykle biography, he said.

The what now? The Mykland biography? I replied and swallowed, placing the jug and glasses down on the kitchen worktop.

Not the case at all, no, he replied.

No?

We barely had a back yard to speak of. I'm just a simple lad from Telemark, he replied before turning around and opening the fridge.

Hilma Ekhult chuckled and held the back of her hand to her mouth. Per Sinding stopped in his tracks and looked at her.

Is there anything you'd like to say, Hilma?

She looked up at him, her hand still covering her mouth, and shook her head.

Kai followed her inside.

I've found a couple of suitable planks, he said cheerfully. I'll sort it out after we've eaten.

Per Sinding turned back to the fridge and grabbed a bottle of white wine, passing it ceremoniously to Kai.

Take a look at that, he said.

A new test, I gathered.

Kai shook his head.

Oh, not for me, thanks. No good for my gut. I can't really handle anything too acidic, Kai said, setting the bottle down on the worktop. I'd love a beer, though, if you've got one.

Per looked at him before bending over with a sigh and fishing a can of beer out of the vegetable drawer. I glanced briefly at the wine label. Meursault.

I, on the other hand, never say no to a burgundy, I said, and Per Sinding glanced at me briefly before fetching three glasses from the cupboard above him and the bottle opener from a drawer that jammed slightly as he closed it.

He opened the bottle with an irritated yank, grabbed a glass and poured a centimetre of wine before passing it to me.

I took the glass from him and swirled the wine around inside it a few times while Per observed me with an expectant, antagonistic expression. I brought the glass to my nose and breathed in deeply, then stopped. The unmistakeable scent of madeira. I glanced up at Per, who looked back at me with a grave expression.

It seems you've been saving this one for a little too long, I said, passing him the glass without another word.

He stuck his nose in the glass and took a deep lungful of air, furrowing his brow.

It's madeirised, I said firmly.

Out of the corner of my eye I caught Hilma Ekhult smiling in a faintly irritated manner, and without a word Per Sinding grabbed the bottle and poured it all down the sink, *glug glug glug*. It took longer than he must have imagined it would – the whole episode lasted some time.

I don't really need any help here, he said sullenly, and placed the bottle in the cupboard under the sink. You can all head on outside.

Of course... Hilma said, smiling apologetically at Kai and me. She turned around and led the way out, all the way to the end of the long table, where she took a seat. We sat opposite her. Hilma Ekhult placed her hat back on her head and sighed almost inaudibly.

Per emerged moments later, this time balancing three tall glasses and an ice bucket like a waiter, he made his way over to us and placed the bucket on the table with a thud, closely followed by the glasses, after which he disappeared inside once again.

Champagne? Hilma murmured as he walked away, before clearing her throat and pouring us both a glass.

Never a bad idea, I said breezily, taking mine.

Kai sat with his can of beer and observed proceedings with a faint smile.

Here's to a wonderful afternoon, I said, and I raised my glass in Hilma's direction.

She smiled her usual tight-lipped smile, and we drank.

Per Sinding's white shirt came into view through the kitchen window, he was moving quickly. Witnessing his many minor setbacks at such close range, so quick to take offence in his very middle-class way, was thrilling. It stood in stark contrast to the public image he had done his best to foster: Per Sinding the radical, the humanist. What's more, he seemed a little too preoccupied with his own appearance for someone of his age.

Without a word Kai got up from the table with his beer in his hand and wandered over to the crooked, ochre-coloured outhouse. The building was almost completely overgrown with ivy and wild honeysuckle, and Kai disappeared inside, emerging moments later with a few long planks of wood under his arm, whistling.

Hilma clearly considered Kai to be a buffer, and was once again visibly uncomfortable to have been left sitting alone with me. She smiled briefly and turned to face the cabin as if to see where the food was, but at that same moment, Per Sinding stuck his head out of the kitchen window.

Five minutes, he called valiantly.

She turned back, and we smiled at one another, slightly embarrassed. She was a classic ice queen: correct, polite, cool.

She gave no indication that she wanted to ask me anything, she wasn't curious about me in the slightest, she'd already found out far more than she wanted to know.

Kai emerged from the outhouse once again, now armed with a crowbar and a hammer.

I cleared my throat.

So, are you working on a book at the moment? I asked eventually, and she looked directly at me.

Never during the summer months.

Why not?

Too hot, too bright,

She shook her head slowly.

The fact that she hadn't written anything for six, almost seven years, I was curious about that, so curious that I had to be careful not to reveal how much I really knew about her.

How long does it take to write a book, then?

It varies. From a few weeks to ... well, to thirty years.

That long, I said, I see. And so, do you write, publish, write, publish, or is there more to it than that?

There are various literary events to attend, lectures, things along those lines.

I see, I said.

Silence resumed between us.

I sipped the cold champagne. I was sweating, wondered why there was no parasol here. Hilma Ekhult sat in the shade of her enormous hat, yet I hadn't even had the forethought to bring a pair of sunglasses.

Even though I was posing purposefully puerile questions, I was immediately filled with rage at her condescending and terse responses. As if I wasn't the sort of person she needed to behave properly around, as if I was more like a moth she could bat away with her delicate hand, her manicured fingernails the same shade as her toes.

I felt it build up within me, but just as I was about the ask a question that might be uncomfortable for her – I still wasn't sure quite what that might be – I was interrupted by a loud crack, Kai had pulled the corner piece loose.

I drank the contents of my glass and ran a hand across my forehead. Hilma gave no indication that she was considering topping up my glass.

So, you and your husband are friendly with the prime minister and his wife, are you? I asked all of a sudden, and she looked at me in surprise.

How did you know that? she asked.

I googled you before we came, I said.

I see, she said.

Do you know what Tony Blair said about his friendship with Gaddafi? I asked.

No, what did he say? she asked, bewildered.

When you reach a certain level, only other heads of state can understand you.

She gazed at me with an expression of cold curiosity.

I reached for the bottle and topped up my own glass.

I see, she replied, did he really?

We heard another crack from Kai's direction as he busied himself with his woodwork.

I said no more. She would have to content herself with a little subtext from my end, too.

Instead she rebuffed me:

Perhaps his comment was what gave you the idea for your segregatory search engine?

She smiled, slowly, with satisfaction.

Quite, I said.

She chuckled, it took me by surprise, each individual 'ha' was clear and distinct.

Per Sinding made his way down the steps, carrying a stack of plates with a white tea towel draped over one of his artificially well-trained forearms, he acted as if he hadn't noticed Kai, who was in the process of breaking up a third rotten plank.

Ladies, he said, lifting the ice bucket and wiping the table as we held our glasses up in the air, then carefully placing the settings.

He turned around, made his way back to the cabin and said something to Kai, who set his tools to one side.

Per Sinding stepped out of the cabin once again, made his way to the table and placed a basket of bread down, along with several small dishes containing pale-green cream.

Hilma's homemade wild-garlic butter, he said proudly, and was rewarded with a smile of feigned embarrassment from Hilma.

Lovely, I said, before Per disappeared once again.

When he emerged for the third time, his expression was solemn. He was carrying an extravagant-looking ovenproof dish from which great plumes of steam unfurled; he placed it down on the table between us.

Langoustine and gruyère gratin, *bon appetit*, he said.

Lovely, and you've even prepped the shellfish for us, I said, sounding peppy.

Wow, Kai said, as he pottered over, his hands freshly washed.

As we ate, I was struck by a bittersweet notion; I regretted not having been more ambitious in my professional life. My entire existence suddenly appeared like a series of comfortable acts of compliance – from stepping down from my position within Iris's royal court, unintentionally making my father the victim of an intricate act of revenge in the process, to choosing to work at the off licence after qualifying as a lawyer with good grades, only then to eventually successfully apply for a laughably lowly role within the local council.

Kai was the only triumph of sorts in my life, and he had appeared as if out of the blue.

Had I not been quite so unambitious in my youth, I might have been a judge by now, or a ruthless, high-profile criminal lawyer. A criminal lawyer and holiday-home owner, because in this fantasy the cabin really *did* belong to us, and there might have been a genuine warmth between us, we might have visited them in Stockholm and had long, quiet conversations, not just about literature and the legal system, that would grow tiresome in the long run, but about real life, difficult decisions, conflicts, dilemmas. Poor judgement and desire, anything you can imagine, and I could be the voice of reason, a criminal lawyer who had seen her fair share of human stupidity, who could act as an advisor and a friend, while Kai could build them bookshelves – how handy it is to have a joiner for a friend. Far more useful than a retired trader, at any rate.

And we could sit together long into the night, here or there, sampling wine and cheese and talking about the complexities of life. Rather than sitting here under a false identity that could be blown at any moment by something as simple as Per Sinding asking me my full name or that of my supposed business.

But we had been safe thus far, and would remain so as long as Per and Hilma continued to behave like the subjects of an interview rather than actual, real-life people; together they awaited our questions, and Per would reply with buzzwords and neat little gems of apparent wisdom, as if he were trapped in a perpetual cycle of questions and answers, while Hilma challenged herself to see just how tight-lipped it was humanely possible to remain.

Each of us was playing a part, four grown adults all playing together, how depressing, and on such a lovely afternoon too. Or at least, three of us were playing – Kai wasn't playing along at all. He sat there with his ankle resting on his left knee, picking at one of his molars and showing very little interest in anything.

A shiver ran through me as I was suddenly struck by the idea that Per might wander over to the neighbouring cabin one bright, warm morning later this summer only to find a completely different couple in residence there. They'd strike up conversation, not to do so would be strange, and slowly the whole situation would unfurl and be revealed for what it truly was. I couldn't bear to think how thrilled Iris would be to hear I'd adorned myself with borrowed plumes.

And do you two have children? I asked impulsively, the thought made me anxious. *Did* they have any children?

A daughter, she's twenty, Per confirmed.

Wow, I said, twenty, and all of a sudden, I could picture her: suntanned, with glossy, light-brown hair, long legs, denim hot pants, I don't know why this H&M ad leapt to mind, but I knew that she was not only beautiful but also an intellectual, no doubt busy studying nutritional biology and continental philosophy.

What's her name? I asked, I didn't really want to know about this astounding daughter of theirs, yet still I asked.

Simone, Per said.

After de Beauvoir or Weil, I reasoned, quick as a flash, it had to be one of the two that Per Sinding and Hilma Ekhult had chosen to name their daughter after.

And she didn't fancy joining her parents on holiday? I asked, and our hosts exchanged a quick glance.

She's back at home in Stockholm, Per said. Things can feel a bit...

Claustrophobic, Hilma said.

Claustrophobic, here? Kai said, glancing out at the sea.

We spend every day together back at home, it seems unfair to bring her here to live at even closer quarters to us, Per said.

She still lives at home then, does she? I asked animatedly.

She stayed at home during the pandemic, Hilma said quickly. But she's moving out after the summer.

We actually want to build a little guest annexe... Per said, trying to change the subject.

That sounds lovely, I said boldly, looking at Hilma.

Per put his cutlery down, rested his nose on his fist and furrowed his brow.

Being parents isn't easy, he said coyly.

I had to stifle a groan, because if there was one thing that was overplayed these days, it was that old chestnut, the 'I haven't been the father I ought to have been' routine, the contrived guilt reserved for uncompromising male artists and explorers.

I really don't see what's so noble about being a bad father, I said.

Noble! Per replied. Hardly the case! That's what makes it so painful.

Hilma sat there in perfect silence, her eyes on the table.

Let's be frank, I said. Your daughter hasn't had just *one*, but *two* parents who've worked from home. There are limits to how absent it's possible to be in such a case.

I'm not talking about *absence*, Per said.

You have to strike a balance, Kai chipped in. Our neighbours work shifts, for example. One sees the kids for a few hours in the afternoon, the other sees them in the mornings, and they never see each other.

Per and Hilma glanced up from their plates and looked over at Kai.

Kai stopped chewing; his eye twitched for a brief moment.

This is it, I thought to myself. We'd warmed up, it had been too easy until now.

Where exactly do you live? Per asked, looking surprised.

Nitt... Kai began.

Skillebekk, I said, interrupting him.

Aha, Per said. It's nice out that way. We've been over there a few times for dinner with Dag and Therese.

Dag and Therese...? Kai asked.

Solstad, Per said. They're good friends of ours.

The author? Dag Solstad lives in Skillebekk? Kai said.

On Drammensveien, Per said.

Trondheimsveien, you mean?

No, Drammensveien.

Skillebekk *in Nittedal*, I said, placing my cutlery down. We live in Skillebekk in Nittedal.

Skillebekk Proper, Kai said, smiling, and Per and Hilma looked at him, bewildered.

You know the old campaign they had, 'Finland Proper', Kai said.

Finland Proper? Per repeated.

You mean you haven't been? Kai said. There's a ferry that goes from Stockholm straight over to Åbo!

Turku, I said, correcting him, they call it Turku. Åbo is what the Swedes call it.

Well, same place, different name, Per said, and he looked as if he'd accepted that we lived in Skillebekk in Nittedal rather than its more fashionable namesake on the west side of Oslo.

Anyway, not to change the subject, Per said, placing his glass down, crossing his legs and preparing to do just that, but we've just inherited some money, and we'd love some advice about investing it.

He looked at Kai and the corners of Hilma's mouth twitched slightly.

So that's why we're here, I thought.

Kai swallowed his food and put down his cutlery.

I know as much as you do on that front, Kai said cheerfully, quickly glancing over at me. There's not really one simple answer to this sort of thing, he continued, and his expression seemed to invite my contribution.

It's hard to advise people, I said. The most important thing is to think long-term.

Hilma Ekhult appeared disconcerted by the swift change of subject.

We really have no idea where to begin, Per said. Where have you invested your money, for example?

He kept turning to look at Kai, which bothered me; if one of us had even the slightest bit of knowledge about these things, it was me.

In stocks and shares, I said.

But which ones, if you don't mind me asking? Per said.

Ha, Kai said. I'm sure you'd like to know.

This is clearly a subject you know a lot about, Per said, still looking at Kai.

If only you knew the truth, Kai said. I've probably lost more than I've ever earned.

How does that even work? Per asked, looking bewildered.

You should speak to someone at your bank, I said. They can advise on that sort of thing.

No, no, no, Per said, shaking his head, convinced we were keeping secrets from him.

You're an author, I said. It's your job to write, not to keep track of the FTSE 100.

I'm sure I can do both! Per Sinding said, throwing out his arms in a resigned manner before calming down once again. Hilma squirmed slightly in her seat next to him.

It was clear that this was some sort of personal, artistic crisis. He was looking for a way out of his quandary. Writing was something he could leave to his wife. He needed a lucrative new line of work, which is to say, he didn't want to work at all, but he *did* want to earn.

The succinct version, I said, is this: you need to decide how big a risk you're willing to take, and that informs you where you should invest your money. The length of time you want to lock your money away for has a big part to play in how big a risk you ought to take. Risk is diminished when you spread your investments, so the higher the risk of any individual investment, the more important it is to spread the rest.

Per listened keenly with an intense look of concentration on his face, but I could tell that he wasn't actually getting the gist of things.

So, what would you recommend? he asked eventually.

I can't really make any recommendations, I said, I'm not acquainted with your situation. I glanced briefly at Hilma, who quickly looked away. But in general, I suppose, an equities fund, perhaps?

I gave a brisk shrug.

Thank you, Per said. Thank you for that.

Hilma Ekhult loosened her grasp on her glass, as if some internal tension had been released and she was at peace once again.

And the higher the risk, the faster the reward? Per interjected, looking up from his food.

Well, yes, but the risk is greater. So, there's a chance you'll lose, rather than win.

He nodded absent-mindedly.

Kai dabbed his chin with his napkin and stood up.

That was a lovely meal, thank you, he said. Let me secure those planks in place before I'm too tipsy to concentrate.

Kai and Per stood down by the jetty, each of them with a can of beer in one hand and a fishing rod in the other. The air was still, even down by the water, small clouds of Per's cigarette smoke billowed up and over his head before dissipating.

I often envied men their uncomplicated ease when it came to hitting their stride with each other. Fragments of quiet conversation and a sudden burst of laughter reached Hilma and me where we were sitting at the long table in the garden. The tree had finally extended its shade over the table, offering us some relief, not something that could be said about the strained atmosphere between myself and Hilma.

I had considered currying favour with her by revealing that I had a greater interest and insight into her affairs and literature and cultural activities than she realised, but it would no doubt only have been an affront to her, she'd want to keep all that to herself.

I regretted having enjoyed her books. I wouldn't have done so if I'd known then what I know now, which is that Hilma Ekhult had taken the need to come across as a fragile genius to absurd lengths.

Reflecting on things now, writing Ibsen-inspired chamber plays in this day and age just seemed conceited.

She always, *always* wrote about upper-class, heterosexual couples. It was evident that she felt a strong affinity with the upper echelons of society. The protagonist in one of her novels was even the CEO of the Central Bank – though I knew now that she'd written that book without the slightest gram of insight into economics or money management.

But she hadn't had anything published in six or seven years. Perhaps she sensed that time and the spirit of an era had run away from her, that she no longer had much to say, not to mention how difficult it must be to enlist new readers.

I started to think that 'being in dialogue with the classics', an aspect of her work for which she was endlessly praised – all of her novels were really just modern-day variations of well-known tragedies – was simply an expression of the fact that she was unable to come up with her own ideas, to craft anything from the ground up, from the inner workings of her own mind.

And the book you're working on now, I said, but before I could finish my question, she held up a hand to stop me in my tracks.

There is no book, she said.

No?

No, she said, and lowered her hand, her expression gloomy.

I realised that she didn't want to talk to me about it, that she considered it entirely meaningless to discuss the process of writing with someone like me; at the same time, it occurred to me that it was someone exactly like me that she really needed, someone with my knowledge of her writing and my general, well, perhaps not *competence*, but *interest* in the field, all concealed behind the fake identity of a cynical tech entrepreneur. Someone like me ought to be able to coax out any problem and zero in on it without hesitation, I was in the perfect position to pinpoint whatever had caused everything to come to a standstill for her, and perhaps even to send her in the right direction.

I get it, I said, but a small twitch at the corner of her mouth revealed that she did not hold the same opinion.

I don't know what things are like in your line of work, but if I know one thing... I began.

She was looking at me now, her gaze analytical, a tad hopeful.

I didn't know what to say. I held my index finger up, tapped my nose.

Follow your nose, I said.

Hilma Ekhult sat there motionless, her brow furrowed.

Follow your nose, I repeated. If you can smell decay and decomposition, that's where you need to be heading.

And is this a principle you follow in your line of work? she asked dryly.

It is, yes. I follow my nose, find those places where the system no longer functions, where it's outdated, the areas that time has forgotten. I go wherever there's something there for the taking. Something that can be transformed and improved upon.

She looked to be mulling over my words.

I can learn something from this person, I thought to myself. This entrepreneur who says what she thinks, who holds eye contact, who commands respect. When we go home, I'm going to take her with me. Maybe this is me, the real me, maybe I've just taken it for granted that I'm someone else, I've taken too many precautions.

Hilma was silent for a good, long while.

I felt certain that she thought it was her own writing that had started to decompose. Her never-ending upper-class intrigues. Positions of power, beautiful homes, expensive wines. Architects, lawyers, politicians and doctors, with the odd artist thrown into the mix, actors and theatre directors, poets, even a sculptor. Anachronistic to the point of parody. It was as if she suddenly realised how trifling it all was as she sat there in front of me.

I'm not sure quite how well that translates to the literary field, she said, with a tight-lipped smile.

Of course it translates, I said. Turn your gaze inwards: what's that bad smell and where is it coming from? *That* should be your starting point.

The look of surprise she gave me was mixed with poorly concealed loathing. She simply couldn't fathom it, the idea that a common entrepreneur had a banal sense of intuition for locating the richest material.

I shrugged.

I'd have thought that were the case, anyway.

The landing net! Kai called out down on the jetty, and Per Sinding scrambled for it.

Hilma Ekhult finally emptied her glass. She was slightly pink-cheeked now, her expression a touch brighter.

I leaned in and poured us both another glass.

There was a book, she said suddenly, her eyes on the sea, which glowed in the evening sunlight.

I said nothing, I'd observed first-hand how holding back often forced someone to carry on talking.

I worked on it for a long time, she continued, her tone flat.

I said nothing.

Down on the jetty, Kai hauled a white fish with a bulging belly from the water.

But then – no.

What happened?

She stretched out a hand, her tiny wrist, took the glass and drank.

She stopped.

Why? I asked.

She remained quiet for a moment; I'd been hoping to open the door a little wider than this.

She took a deep breath, looked away.

The editor I'd worked with for years died.

...A natural death? I asked, hoping for a little mystery.

A blood clot, she said, putting a swift end to that debate.

But you must have been assigned a new one, surely?

She turned and looked at me with disdain. Clearly I didn't understand the pivotal role of the editor.

Yes, some young... she began, then stopped, regretting entering into this discussion in the first place.

I could picture the scene. A young, newly appointed editor, reverent yet also keen to improve things, had come along and taken on the editing of Hilma Ekhult's work, daring to question the white heteronormativity that permeated her books, the socioeconomic homogeny, the absence of any diversity whatsoever, to be frank.

What was the issue? I asked.

He was an idiot, Hilma Ekhult replied, short and sweet.

I see, I said.

I picked up my glass and took a sip, waiting for her to continue, but Hilma Ekhult simply gazed into the distance, stock-still.

Surely you could have switched publisher if you were unhappy? I said eventually.

She smiled condescendingly without looking at me.

No?

It's not quite that simple, she said.

Get someone else to read it, I said. Get a second opinion.

I was surprised at how easily fazed she was. A new editor was all it took to knock her off course? She must be more plagued with doubt than her success would suggest.

Let me read it, I said suddenly.

She laughed, spontaneous and sincere.

No, she said, solemn once again. It's all in the past now.

How can it be when you can't move forward? I asked.

She sighed.

The horizon unfolded behind her, the tiny islands further out, small boats shuttling back and forth.

What's it about? I asked encouragingly.

She sighed silently, demonstrating her unwillingness to reply to such a trivial question.

Come on, I'm interested, I said.

About an artist who returns to the town she grew up in.

OK, I said earnestly. Exciting stuff! And?

No, well, she said, gazing into the distance. She gave a resigned smile, then turned to look at me.

Tell me, I said.

She's been tasked with painting a mural in the stairwell of the new district court, but then...

She stopped. Suddenly realised that she was sitting here explaining the plot of an artistic novel to some random investor.

Life's much simpler for you, she said. You only have one objective. To maximise profit.

Well... I said.

But for me, she said. I don't know what the goal *is*, whether it even exists, and the harder I try to meet that goal, the more it eludes me.

The self-pity she exuded was new to me. I felt unsure how I ought to respond to her. I couldn't work out if she was looking for advice or simply trying to articulate the unique and agonising pain of life as an artist, something she supposed I could never understand.

She smiled bitterly.

Let me read your book, I repeated. I'm sure it's...

The book isn't the problem, she said. The book is good.

So, what *is* the problem?

She sighed yet again, her silhouette clear-cut against the backdrop of the evening sun.

No... she said.

So you didn't receive a standing ovation for the first time in your life? Is that the problem here? I blurted out, and even as I uttered the words I was astounded at myself; her jaw tensed.

You don't understand, she said.

No, I said, I'm sure I don't. And you won't explain.

Silence fell between us yet again.

You may or may not believe it, but I read a lot, I said.

Oh yes? she said, looking directly at me, and though her expression wasn't overtly scornful, it was there beneath the surface, in her face and in her tone. I could picture the books she imagined I read: a cheerful combination of airport paperbacks and Ayn Rand.

She grabbed her glass and downed the contents.

Get the manuscript back out, I said. Insist on having a new editor.

I haven't looked at it for at least five years, she said. I don't even know if I still have it.

Of course you still have it, I said. It'll be in your email outbox.

The internet out here is— she began, but I interrupted her.

But if you want to allow some arrogant, inexperienced whippersnapper to destroy your career, that's your choice, I said breezily. If I'd allowed any cocky old git to stand in my way, I wouldn't be where I am today. I thought you were a feminist?

Kai and Per left the jetty and strolled in our direction.

Hilma pulled her shawl up around her shoulders.

Bouillabaisse for dinner, Per announced, proudly showing off the bucket containing his catch.

There was blood on Kai's shirt and his wrist glistened, the shimmer of fish scales.

Time for me to retire, Hilma said, standing up.

I'd been careless, offended her, and now she intended to punish me for it.

Time for us to head off too, I said.

Not yet, surely? Per said.

He gazed at Kai somewhat pleadingly, who looked at me with the same expression.

Let me finish my beer, at least, Kai said, sitting beside me.

Thank you for coming, Hilma said, and started making her way towards the cabin.

I'll stick some coffee on, Per said, following her up with the bucket in his hand.

And what, pray tell, have you two been debating down there? I asked, and Kai popped one of Per's cigarettes between his lips.

Has he got you smoking now, too? I asked.

Do you want one?

No thank you, I replied, then helped myself to a swig of his beer instead.

Bit of fun, isn't it, being someone else? he said, lighting his cigarette.

Fun, but not without its risks, I said.

Not with these two, Kai said. They couldn't be any less curious about us if they tried.

He glanced back at the cabin.

He hasn't asked me a single question, you know, not one, he murmured.

She's the same, I said.

All he wants are investment tips.

I turned to look at him.

He's still going on about that? I asked.

It's alright, I'm getting the hang of it, he said. It makes sense, when you think about it. You just need to buy before everyone else, then sell before they do.

You haven't been talking to him about stocks and shares? I said.

He took a drag of his cigarette and the end crackled and glowed.

Kai! I hissed. You can't go messing around with other people's money.

He gazed into the distance and slowly exhaled, the smoke billowing around us.

I gave him a long, hard stare.

I had to say something, he said. I can't just draw a blank whenever he asks me for advice.

So, what exactly did you say?

Well, timber, for instance, it's very expensive these days, but it'll be cheap again before too long. So that might be worth investing in.

Wait, *what*? It's not the price of *goods* that matters, Kai, this is stocks and shares we're talking about. It's the opposite way around, you're supposed to buy *cheap*!

He looked at me, perplexed.

You advised him to invest in *timber*?

It was just a suggestion, Kai said meekly.

I started to feel faint.

He burst out laughing.

I'm joking, he said.

My God, I said, clutching my chest with one hand.

He shook his head.

Surely you don't think I'm *that* stupid, he said.

You *are* stupid, I retorted.

He stumped out his cigarette in the grass and chucked the butt under a bush behind us.

So they've inherited money, but they need a quick return? I said slowly. That doesn't ... wait.

What? he said.

They're broke, I said.

Broke? Kai repeated. Hardly, take a look around you.

She hasn't had anything published for seven years now, I said. And he isn't earning a penny.

I looked at him.

Rotten wood panelling, I said. And the burgundy. They'd been saving it for so long that it'd gone off.

I pulled out my phone and glanced up at the cabin, then went into the free public database of personal details, searched for Hilma and found the address for her Swedish home. A grey, built-up area with huge, criss-crossing roads, far, far away from trendy Södermalm and the other sophisticated streets of Stockholm.

You know why they live in Stockholm? I said. It's because they can't afford to live in Oslo!

Stockholm is hardly Skid Row, Kai said.

I held the screen up to show Kai.

There! I said. They live *there*, in the middle of some sort of ... ghetto.

He took my phone and squinted at the map, but I grabbed it back from him and did an image search for photographs of Hilma Ekhult, and every single interview she'd given in Stockholm had taken place in a park or a museum café or a restaurant in a fashionable part of town, all miles away from her actual home address. She hadn't given a single interview at home, in the hovel in which they *actually* resided.

All this talk of shabby chic, I said, when really it's just ... *shabby*.

But they can't have any money to invest if they're hard up, Kai said.

They need money fast, I said. That's why we're here.

Per Sinding's brown legs appeared in the doorway. He was carrying a tray and making a beeline for us.

We should have left when we had the chance, I whispered to Kai.

So there's no inheritance money after all? Kai whispered as Per approached us.

No inheritance money, I said.

But what about this place?

This is the inheritance.

Per set out delicate little porcelain cups, a cafetière and a small plate of macarons – macarons! I thought to myself, is he having us on, is that the kind of thing he thinks people of our calibre like? Quite suddenly it was as if I could see everything so clearly, all the groundwork he'd put into this supposedly inconsequential little late lunch, the langoustines given to them by a friend, the champagne, they'd taken the boat out just to buy pale-pink and yellow and green macarons for us, it was all so desperate. Had Hilma been out foraging for wild garlic just to save a few pennies?

I felt a sudden pang of pity for them both. Per Sinding's unsuccessful career, and Hilma Ekhult's writer's block, triggered by the most minor of setbacks.

Per Sinding poured our coffee with a placid expression, grateful smile lines gathering at the corners of his eyes.

I brought my coffee cup to my lips and took a sip.

The sun was still warm, even though it had to be pushing eight o'clock. I felt a faint sense of infinitude, no doubt prompted by the alcohol and the soothing sounds of the sea. A distant clucking sound, the drone of engines, merged into the ubiquitous sea breeze.

Do you happen to have a card on you, in case I need a little advice down the line? Per asked. In terms of investments, I mean.

A card? Not on me, no, Kai said.

OK, your number then, perhaps.

Kai shook his head firmly.

I've known you, what, three hours? I'm afraid I don't go handing my phone number out willy-nilly.

Per grinned, but then he looked uncertain, glancing quickly at me, then at Kai.

Seriously?

Kai maintained his mask.

Sorry. That's not how it works.

Per lifted his hands in the air, palms facing us.

No, no, of course, sorry.

That's fine, Kai said. But this isn't a game for me.

No, of course, Per said. He lifted his coffee cup and drank.

I was impressed by Kai's naturally superior mannerisms when he was in character. It wasn't the simplest of roles, but there was a strong element of mystery to draw upon. No end of unwritten rules and obstacles that Per might come up against in his hunt for a quick return on his investment.

Per took a pale-yellow macaron, gently holding it in his increasingly tragicomic athletic hand, and once again I felt pity for him. Pity for the fact that we were tricking him, to put things bluntly. We mocked him to his face, and suddenly I couldn't recall what had made all this so necessary in the first place, what exactly had justified this trickery, was it because Per had said the words 'private property' that day, was that what had been so unbearable? What did that say about me? It was a straightforward statement, not an attempt to strip me of my humanity.

And then later, the fact Per had looked at us so oddly as we'd made our way towards the cabin, as if he'd doubted we were the real owners. He was right! There was no getting away from it.

My coffee had gone cold in the almost weightless

porcelain cup, which felt many sizes too small for my hands; it was much better suited to Hilma Ekhult's delicate touch.

I hadn't been to the toilet since we'd arrived, I was sure that I'd manage to wait until we got back home, but we hadn't left for home, and the time had come.

I stood up.

The loo? I asked.

Inside and first on the right, Per replied.

I crossed the lawn and made my way inside, along the creaky, crooked hallway and to the right. The door was painted light grey, the handle black, and the room itself was a tight space but pleasant enough, with a strong, spicy scent that emanated from a pot on the windowsill.

I helped myself to a glass of water in the kitchen, which I drank as I looked out at the two men.

It occurred to me that Per Sinding was a man with few, if any, friends, not close ones at any rate. But that was a good starting point for a friendship with us, particularly with Kai, who was neither particularly interested in himself nor in others; he was who he was.

Where was Hilma at this point? I turned around. The kitchen was downstairs, along with the bathroom and a sitting room, not much more than that, as far as I could tell.

She must be upstairs, there might be a few bedrooms up there, one of them fitted out with a desk, perhaps.

I placed my glass on the worktop and carefully made my way into the hall. I could hear sounds from upstairs, and I stopped in my tracks. A soft clicking. Hesitantly I placed my foot on the bottom step, cautiously putting my weight on it bit-by-bit to see if the stair would creak, but there wasn't a sound. I took one step, then did the same again with the next step, and the one after that, until I was five steps up, my eyes level with the upstairs floor. I looked from left to right, saw a door at each end, as I'd expected, and one of them was ajar. It was her. I could hear the clacking of fingers on a keyboard.

Slow, steady taps, considered and contemplative, I felt sure of it. Then she stopped, and I froze. Everything fell silent, she must have sensed my presence.

I stood there on the fifth step, stock-still, not daring to breathe.

Then the silence was broken by the unmistakeable hum of a printer starting up.

I crept back downstairs, the hum of the printer concealing any sound I might make, then silently sneaked out of the door and returned to Kai and Per at the long table.

I awoke to see Kai bringing me a steaming mug of coffee.

I sat up and took the mug.

Light flooded into the room. I grabbed my phone from the bedside table, it was ten o'clock.

What do you fancy for breakfast? he asked me, perching on the bed next to me.

Can't we just get out of here, get something to eat on the way home? I asked.

Don't you think we should spend time here by the coast rather than stuck in the van? It's a gorgeous day.

I thought I'd won this argument, I said crossly.

Fine, he said, sounding vexed and getting up. I'll clean the bathroom.

I'm sure a cleaner will be coming in after we leave, I called after him, but he was already gone.

I stood up, pulled on the clothes I'd worn yesterday and made my way into the living room. I filled the kitchen sink with hot water, added some detergent and traipsed off to find a broom.

Cleaning up after ourselves took two hours, the sun flooded the cabin with ruthless intent, illuminating every speck of dirt on the various smooth surfaces. Eventually I washed each of the coffee cups by hand, dried them, took one last look at the rooms and grabbed my suitcase.

Just as I closed the door behind me and heard the metallic click of the lock, I spotted a figure: Per Sinding's salt-and-pepper locks and forehead popped up from behind the rock just west of the cabin.

Well look at you two early birds, he said as he strolled over with his hands in the pockets of his light-brown shorts.

Hi there, I said, in a more leisurely manner than felt strictly natural.

Per stopped, glanced down at the suitcase in my hand and looked around for Kai.

What's going on? he asked.

I need to pop into the office, I said.

What about Kai?

Kai's coming with me, I said. He's going ... golfing.

Where is he now?

Kai was sitting in the van twenty metres away, hidden just behind the rock. The orange van with its big, black letters: *Kai Braaten Joinery*.

He's ... down there, locking up the boat, I mumbled.

Oh, Per said. Were you really going to leave without saying goodbye?

It's just a brief trip back, I said.

I stood there with my suitcase on wheels, didn't know where to go.

To the office? Per said. There was me thinking everything was digital these days. Has something happened? You're not cancelling your holiday, I hope?

Everything's fine, I said. I just need to deal with a few things.

Hmm, Per said.

Then Kai ambled onto the scene, not from the direction of the water, but from where we'd parked the van, and Per looked up.

Golfing, eh? he said. What's your handicap?

Frisbee golf, actually, Kai said.

I just explained to Per that I've got to pop back to work briefly, I said, making sure to enunciate myself very clearly.

Yes, Kai said, you know how it is, there's always something. But we'll be back.

I have to know, what was it you said to her? Per asked me, crossing his arms.

I ... I'm not sure I know what you mean, I said, bewildered.

He held my gaze.

Nothing in particular, I said.

It was then that I noticed he was clutching a charcoal-grey, marble-patterned file in one hand.

Why do you ask?

She didn't come to bed until three o'clock in the morning, Per said. She'd been working for seven hours straight. And now...

Now? I said.

Hilma never lets anyone read her work. But this is a new era. She's wondering if you'd... Per stopped himself mid-flow.

Well, not *wondering*, he went on, correcting himself. She's very keen that you should read it.

He held the file out, waiting for me to take it.

Me? I said. What does she need *me* for?

He shrugged.

You must have a good nose for this sort of thing. You proved that yesterday, whatever it was you said to her.

Kai looked at me with a smug smile on his face.

It'll only take a few hours, Per said, reaching out further, the ring binder edging ever closer, it's quite short, as you can see.

I set my suitcase down, couldn't speak.

Sit yourself down in the sun, he said, glancing up at the house, it won't be setting for a while yet, have a read, relax. Then Hilma can swing by for a chat later on.

Here? I said. Today?

Mhmm? Shall we say this evening? Per said.

I shook my head.

I can't. I really need to get back.

Push it back by one day, Per said.

Karin, Kai said, stepping in. This is an honour.

It is, of course it is... I said. But...

Hot off the press, Per said, placing the printout in my hands. It's still warm.

He stepped back and I stood there with the folder in my hand; it didn't feel that warm to me.

We'll pop by around seven, he said.

I looked over at Kai.

Lovely, Per said, ever the dutiful errand boy, and he turned tail elegantly and began the stroll back home.

I waited for him to disappear out of sight before letting out a heavy sigh.

What? Kai said.

We were milliseconds away from escaping!

There's no reason for us to hurry home, he said. We get to enjoy another day out here, it's neither here nor there. We don't need to be back until tomorrow.

We had both agreed we were going home, I said, grabbing my suitcase, I started making my way back towards the cabin.

Isn't it nice, you know, the fact that they're coming over here to see us? Kai said.

Have you forgotten, I said, taking a deep breath to calm

myself down, that they think we're two completely different people? They're *this close* to discovering who we really are!

Then let's just be honest, Kai said serenely. What are they going to do? Turn around and leave because we're not rich after all? They enjoy our company, and we enjoy theirs, that's all that really matters.

We've lied to their faces for days on end.

They might find the whole thing funny, you never know, Kai called after me, and I closed my eyes, mumbling under my breath as I shook my head.

Can't you just make the most of the holiday? he said. This is our only trip away this summer, and you want to go home? Do you realise how much people pay to spend a week in a place like this?

Make the most of it? Of *what*? I said, stopping by the front door.

What's wrong with you, Karin? You were having dinner with your favourite author yesterday...

Late lunch, I said, correcting him.

...*late lunch* with your favourite author, *and* you've inspired her to write again, *and* she's coming to visit you this evening to hear your thoughts on her latest novel, what more could you ask for?

She's not visiting *me*, I said, she's visiting someone else entirely.

They like us, Kai said with a shrug. I enjoyed yesterday, for what it's worth.

I said nothing.

You can enjoy being here even if it doesn't belong to you, you know, Kai said eventually.

No, I said, throwing out my arms, I can't! *You* can enjoy being here, this isn't in any way complicated for you, you can go fishing and do whatever you fancy, but I...

What?

It's just a reminder of everything I don't have, I said.

But you don't even *want* all this. You told me yourself that you want a cabin in the mountains with a wood-burning stove.

I *do*! I shouted. Of course I do.

So, if this place didn't happen to belong to your childhood nemesis, if this was just a random cabin I'd found on Airbnb, Kai said, would that make it OK?

She wasn't my nemesis, I said.

Would that make it OK? he repeated.

Yes, I said eventually, sounding sullen.

OK, I hadn't realised you're actually thirteen years old, Kai said, sounding resigned, he shook his head and I could understand where he was coming from, but I don't think he understood where *I* was coming from.

I'm going to take the boat out one last time, Kai said, waiting.

Fine, I said.

Fine, he replied, and I pulled out my phone and let myself back into the cabin. I placed the manuscript on the kitchen worktop and slipped off my shoes.

I plugged the coffee machine back in, helped myself to a glass of water and found a pencil at the bottom of my bag. I made myself a cup of coffee and took the manuscript over to one of the occasional chairs, I think that's what they call them anyway, who knows, but either way, it had a wall-to-wall view out over the Skagerrak strait and the vast sky above.

I couldn't understand it. She had walked off looking indignant in response to my innocent remark about her being a bad feminist, and now she wanted to treat me like some sort of consultant? Simply because they needed the money? She planned to scrounge off my entrepreneurial nose for profit, and I was going to market-analyse her manuscript and advise her on how to make it more marketable?

Or was Hilma Ekhult labouring under the more or less irrational misapprehension that I had some sort of 'pure', impartial insight, that I was some sort of literary *noble savage*?

No matter how great an honour it might be, it was an honour addressed to a fictional entrepreneur and not to *me*, a vaguely neurotic mother of two and consultant for Nittedal county council.

Nevertheless, I *could* have been someone else, I thought to myself, if it hadn't been for Iris holding me back, or worse: causing me to hold *myself* back. I could have been in Hilma Ekhult's league, fraternising with members of parliament and supreme court justices, my imagination ran riot as I opened the folder and leafed through the pages, I pictured the kind of scene that might feature in a future literary history or perhaps a biography of Hilma Ekhult's life, the moment that a mysterious, anonymous consultant read and commented on what would become Hilma Ekhult's famous comeback novel after it had wallowed at the bottom of a drawer for seven years, a whimsical woman without a name or a face, just someone that Hilma Ekhult happened to meet one sunny day by the Oslo fjord in the summer of 2022, and who she never saw again.

The first page was blank. I carried on turning the pages, feeling a glimmer of hope that I might spot a 'To Karin' in there, but the next page was also blank, and then came the title in modest-sized lettering on the third page: *Pentimento*. Straight away I pencilled my first minus sign in the margin. Too pompous. I checked the last sheet to see exactly how many pages she expected me to plough my way through by this evening. Just 120. A novella. That ought to be manageable.

I had started to fear that this was all a bad joke – that she had written an entire book overnight all about how she and Per had fallen victim to a couple with an inferiority complex pretending to be rich and successful, a sharp and accurate account of our helpless attempts to come across as more impressive than we actually were, the first book in which

Hilma Ekhult demonstrated a finely tuned sense of humour, a feature that hadn't necessarily loomed large in her earlier novels – but after a few pages it became clear to me that the novel was about exactly what she'd told me it was about: an artist who reluctantly returns to her hometown to paint a mural in the new district-court stairwell.

Her cool, elevated prose was her trademark; stringent yet impactful, it filled the pages.

She effectively established a sense of intrigue between the female artist, her bourgeois sister, who now lived in their childhood home, and her husband; I was immediately captivated.

The artist only works in the evenings, in darkness, to quash the critical voices in her head. She is plagued by doubt about her own abilities. She dreams of creating something with genuine impact, yet she is best known for her mellow Anni Albers-inspired paintings, all of which resemble tea towels but which sell well in upper-middle-class circles.

I reached page eighteen and placed the manuscript down, glancing at the clock. One hour. It had taken me one hour to read eighteen pages. I'd been making numerous notes in the margin, small exclamation marks and plus signs here and there, but how would that help Hilma Ekhult?

I felt a sense of awe. Entirely natural, of course. This was a Hilma Ekhult novel, after all. Her novels formed the basis of many a doctorate degree. She would be going on tour to promote this novel, when it was eventually published, it would be translated into countless languages and distributed across every continent.

And here was I, sitting with that very book in my hands, and I'd been offered a pivotal role in its creation.

She was surrounded by people unwilling to contradict her, nobody dared offer a real opinion for fear of violating her fragile ego, something that she knew only too well.

I suddenly realised how hungry I was. The bag we'd filled with our leftovers was by my suitcase, half a box of eggs, half a pack of butter, the rest of a loaf of walnut bread. I filled a pan with water, placed it on the hob and pricked holes in two eggs.

This evening, it suddenly occurred to me, what in heaven's name would we serve them this evening?

The prospect of more seafood made me feel ill. Just a simple casserole! A beef bourguignon! If we were having guests over on a balmy June evening at home I'd serve cured meat and home-baked flatbread, my special potato salad and wheat beer to drink, just something simple but delicious. But we were all hostage to the holy church of seafood on this

Vatican peninsula, lukewarm saltwater and lumpfish offered up for Holy Communion.

I pulled out my phone and started writing up a shopping list while my eggs were boiling. If Kai took the boat along the coastline and into town within the next few hours, he'd make it to the off licence well before it closed at six, I thought to myself, but if Hilma and Per were due to come at seven then we'd have to go for something simple, a warm quiche and a simple salad, maybe, something like that – and then I realised it was Saturday. The off licence always closed at three on Saturdays. I glanced at the clock: half past two.

No, no, no, I muttered out loud.

Kai didn't pick up his phone, and so I tried again. As it continued to ring, a hollow feeling gripped me, and I marched towards the window to see if I could spot him out on the water. I opened the glass door and looked out to sea, the fact that his phone was ringing was probably a good sign, he hadn't ended up overboard that way, at least?

I stepped outside and made my way to the front of the cabin, kept my eyes peeled for a medium-sized white boat, but all the boats out here were medium-sized and white in colour, it was impossible to distinguish one from another.

I made my way back inside, glanced at the clock once again. He wouldn't make it in time. We'd have to skip the drinks, if that wasn't a completely absurd concept. Perhaps we could empty Iris's drinks cabinet, serve a number of improvised vodka-based beverages.

I took the pan of water off the heat and rinsed the eggs under cold water, cut two slices of bread and fetched a plate, grabbed the manuscript and sat at the kitchen island. I forced myself to read on as I ate, but I kept trying to call Kai all the while, and with every unsuccessful attempt I reluctantly imagined various scenarios. He had fallen overboard with his phone still in the boat, or maybe it was still back on land, for that matter.

But he was such a strong swimmer, could it be something to do with his heart?

I was aware of my thoughts running away with me, yet unable to stop them in their tracks; I chewed my food and pictured myself as a widow dressed in black with a front-row seat, silent and dignified, like a stone statue, a boy on each side of me, Kai's parents inconsolable, his sister completely falling apart. I tried calling him again, my heart hammered in my chest, it dawned on me that I'd make a terrible single mother, and still he failed to pick up his phone.

The boys. I'd have to do my best to be as strict with them as Kai was. Homework, jobs, personal hygiene, I'd have to rally whatever reserves I had to keep things as they were, even if it meant letting other things slide.

Kai tended to be the one who took them to their extra-curricular activities, because on the occasions that I did go, I was fixated on making sure the other children included them to a manic degree, my own irreversible impairment, and one that I'd pass directly onto them if nobody was around to stop me. And Kai *was* there to stop me, but would it now fall to me to take our eldest to football practice every other week, to stand on the side lines and radiate maternal insecurity?

I'd already gone through imaginary therapy for this for many years. I'd envisaged myself telling an imaginary psychologist all about my upbringing and how it had affected me as a mother, and my imaginary psychologist had advised me on what to do, and although this advice was always sensible, concrete and uncomplicated, I could never quite trust it given that it had come from me.

I didn't need to stand there, I thought to myself, focused on finding solutions, I could drive him there and then take his brother to the library or a playpark before returning to collect him afterwards.

I drank half a glass of water, realised it was too late, they had already inherited too much from me.

I picked up the phone and took it outside with me once again, jogged down the steps to the jetty, the tone still ringing in my ear.

The boat was gone.

Both the boys and I needed Kai for his drive, I thought, looking out to sea. I wouldn't be able to give the boys the confidence they needed to survive in society. Not without Kai. I'd turn them into victims of never-ending self-scrutiny, I'd infect them with my solipsism. The eldest was showing small signs of it already, by the time he started nursery he'd already developed a disarming giggle and could still pull a baby voice out of the bag when he was nervous.

I ran back up the steps towards the cabin and it struck me that there would be an end to Kai's exaggerated approach to laundry, at the very least. He washed everything after one wear, he was obsessed with clean clothes, even when it came to his working wardrobe. There was always a towering pile of dirty clothes at home and endless damp laundry hanging up to dry, taking up all the space in the house, the machine was constantly on the go.

That didn't make up for the fact he'd be lost to us forevermore, obviously. But it wasn't like him to fall overboard. Kai was so cautious. I'd never seen him stumble. As for me, on the other hand, I'd barely had the confidence to hold my eldest for fear of dropping him as a baby, even when I was sitting down, yet Kai had carried him around, up and down stairs, always so relaxed, rocking him to sleep, and I had trusted him completely.

Ergo, it must have been another boat that had crashed into him, I reasoned, or one of those terrifying jet skis. Or even more likely than that: he'd come across the wreckage of another boat, someone had hit the rocks, and now he was preoccupied with saving lives and unable to pick up the phone.

When I got back up to the cabin, all these various scenarios running through my head, I became aware of a faint, familiar sound that grew louder as I rounded the corner. I let out a heavy sigh when I spotted his bag on the steps.

It was the type of relief that very quickly turns to irritation as I realised that it was now impossible for me to ask Kai to go shopping for this evening's supplies. It would mean that I had to take the van into town all by myself, and not just any old town, but the very centre of a summer holiday hotspot in the last week of June, filled as it would be with tanned, athletic boating types, wealthy folks with their sunglasses pushed up on top of their heads; I'd have to manoeuvre my way around them until I finally found a parking space, then I'd have to wrap my head around the parking payment system without drawing attention to myself, and *then* I'd have to dawdle around the shops, completely unaware of what to buy and where to get it, staggering, stiff-legged, lugging heavy bags, beer bottles clattering inside them, given that other options were off the table what with the off licence already being closed for the day, sweat trickling down my face, only to transport everything back to the huge vehicle and manoeuvre my way back out of the car park again. All these tasks that were so straightforward for Kai, *so* straightforward, and yet so problematic for me.

Feeling vexed, I opened one of the side pockets of his bag and pulled out his phone, which showed eleven missed calls from me and a text from an unknown number. I took the phone inside and placed it on the kitchen worktop with a feigned groan when a vague sense of the familiar caused me to glance at the screen once again. An icy talon clawed at my guts when I caught sight of the unknown number; it was identical to one on my own phone. I fetched my phone to double-check, and there it was, digit for digit. It was the same number.

Kai had received a text from Iris Vilden.

I hadn't given her his number. I had acted as middle-woman for any contact between them. She didn't even know his surname.

I took a deep breath to quieten everything that was beginning to build up inside me. His name was listed at the same address as mine. His number was in the public domain. It was nothing, hardly strange at all that anyone would be in touch with the joiner doing work for them.

I'd known his pin code once upon a time, we'd had the same one, our eldest's birthday. But at some point in time Kai had changed his pin, it might have been about a month since I'd failed to unlock his phone when I'd tried to check the weather one day.

I'd asked him about it. Have you changed your pin code? What had he said?

I tried the old code, tapped it in without daring to breathe, it was wrong.

Without thinking, I tried our youngest's birthday – and his phone unlocked.

With my thumb trembling, I tapped on the text message from Iris. There it was: *Great*, followed by a heart and a stupid, sunglasses-wearing smiley.

It was the only message in any correspondence between them. Which is to say, there was no correspondence. I knew what that meant, the fact that the only message between them was the one on the screen in front of me. It meant that he was deleting any messages as he went.

I sat at the kitchen island, felt the weight of his phone in my hand. He had sent a text to his employer. Job done, for instance. His employer had replied to say that this was good news. That was hardly unusual. What *was* unusual was that he had deleted the message that Iris had replied to. The second unusual thing was that he hadn't asked me for her number. But was that unusual? Perhaps not, after what I'd told him about her.

I cleared my plate. Then I grabbed his phone again, the weather and news were the only open apps. The news app only showed a few newspaper headlines.

What else did he have? Neither of us used social media. The closest he came to using social media was YouTube, he would watch Japanese furniture-making videos when he was downstairs in his cellar workshop.

I opened his emails, searched 'Vilden', nothing. Searched 'Wexøe'. Nothing.

I shouldn't be snooping like this. I had to ask him outright. Or simply say: Oh, you got a text from Iris, by the way, and analyse his reaction.

I opened his call log and clutched a theatrical hand to my chest.

Her number was top of the list.

He had called her today, while I had been sleeping.

My heart began to pound in my chest, I could feel the vibration all the way down to the base of my spine.

While I was *sleeping*.

The conversation had lasted almost four minutes. What exactly did they have to talk about for *four minutes*? Arranging for the disposal of any waste, that would be thirty seconds max, the details of any invoicing, that would be fifteen seconds at most, thanks for doing such a good job, ten seconds, what exactly had they talked about for the remaining *three minutes*?

I checked the rest of his call log; he'd called his parents before he'd spoken to her. Spoken to the boys, no doubt.

There were a couple of missed calls from unknown numbers under that, and then, yesterday morning: another call from her. I glanced at the time.

It was the call he'd taken after we'd been swimming, when we'd had breakfast and kissed and his phone had rung, when he'd taken it with him outside.

I felt a weight on my chest, in my throat.

It was so obvious, it hit me all of a sudden. There had been something odd that I hadn't quite been able to put my finger on. The way he'd asked me to navigate on our way here, but hadn't asked me for any actual directions even once. The way he'd found his way around this labyrinth of a kitchen without any difficulty.

He acted as if he were at home here.

He had been here before.

Was she somewhere nearby? In another cabin? Had they met one day when I was wandering around at a loose end, my skin burning in the summer sun like some sort of idiot? Was it some sort of game they were playing, did they like meeting up like this, did it feel dangerous, did they enjoy the idea of me in the background, an oblivious onlooker?

I shook my head, no, no, this is nonsense, I'd always been like this, prone to destructive patterns of thinking at the earliest opportunity, my negative assumptions ran away with me. I gulped down my glass of water, tried to cool my head, opened my mouth as widely as I could to relax my muscles.

Then it all hit me once again.

The way we'd just so happened to bump into Iris that evening in the pub, the pub that Kai had suggested we visit in the first place.

I let out a cold chuckle. Iris and Kai – what did they have in common? What on earth did a woman like her see in a man like him? Kai, with his shaggy, red beard, a living, breathing cultural desert, he didn't have a single clue about the world she floated around in.

I slipped down from the bar stool and made my way over to the family portrait hanging on the wall.

There she was, Iris, an inconsiderate, bacchanal woman, permanently in pursuit of risk, fever, ecstasy. A man like Kai couldn't provide her with any of those things.

And then there was Mikkel Wexøe. Young, handsome, wealthy and media-shy. Strong, brown arms, cold, blue eyes. Renewable energy and a disdain for weakness. They deserved one another.

Who was Kai, pitted against this man? I mulled over it with some relief until it hit me.

It was so simple, so obvious when the realisation hit you.

Who was Kai? He was mine.

I knew I was being dramatic. I wanted to grab my bag, my suitcase, my shoes, to stamp out of the door and slam it closed behind me. To climb up the rocks, along the path and up to the van, to pull the driver's door open and drive away. All the way to Son, where I'd tear the boys out of my in-laws' clutches, put them in the car, drive them home, stick a big box under the bedroom window and chuck his things straight into it.

That wasn't a mature way of dealing with things, but this was the kind of situation that permitted a level of immaturity.

That was why he was so eager to stay, because he was off meeting Iris somewhere nearby. Was he there now, with her, while I was here?

How could he do that to the boys, take away the only advantage they had in life: the fact that they were part of something as simple and sad as a traditional nuclear family, rather than the offspring of a divorced couple? Although whether or not that was actually an advantage was up for discussion.

There was still a chance that this was all in my head, I tried telling myself, my thoughts had a tendency to run away from me, eventually spiralling off the nearest cliff.

He had called her, but there could be a simple explanation for that.

The fact that he'd met her that evening, that could be a coincidence.

Him having been here before? Kai was like a wolf when it came to navigation, he was well acquainted with huge stretches of the east coast, not least the Oslo fjord, he'd worked all over the place, wherever there were people, there was work.

I had to ask him outright. But I knew he'd deny it. So how could I coax it out of him, if there was even anything to coax out? How could I make him explain the reason for their phone calls? I couldn't imagine Kai being a decent liar. He'd either break down and confess everything or serve up a highly plausible, and true, explanation.

Breathe in, breathe out, and repeat, I told myself, in through the nose and out through the mouth, I closed my eyes and held myself steady, with the help of the wall by the family portrait.

I want to go home, I thought to myself once again, why weren't we on our way home? Weren't we supposed to be going home? Then I looked at the manuscript. It was lying in two piles on the dining table, and I'd only made it to page eighteen.

I felt like a defective pressure cooker. I tried to nurture my rage at the fact that it was me who now had to go food shopping to prepare for the visit, who had to make dinner, as well as race through my favourite author's manuscript, which had been presented to me as an important task, a great honour, and all while Kai was out at sea, bobbing along with his fishing rod, enjoying a semi-secret exchange with the person who'd had such a negative impact on my life. But I only felt weak, empty, my shoulders and neck ached.

I sat back in my chair, picked up the manuscript and pencil, and continued to read about the self-critical artist. I made it through half a page before picking up my phone and searching Iris's address in Oslo. I wanted to see where she lived. I wondered if it was possible to track Kai's movements somehow, to see if he'd been to her house before.

The house was on Admiral Børresens vei on Bygdøy peninsula, with its own stretch of beach and a jetty. Honestly, I said, muttering out loud, chuckling slightly. I loathed the idea of her two little boys, no doubt the recipients of private tennis tuition when my two had never even held a racquet. Iris sitting there in her white dressing gown, sipping champagne outside her tiny bathhouse along with her actress friends – but what on earth do they talk about? I wondered. Superficial nonsense! Handbags and chemical peels! But then I stopped, because what did *I* talk about? What was it that I spent *my* life doing?

For my sixth birthday, I'd requested – and received! – a Mozart cassette tape, no word of a lie. I had loved to paint. Music had meant everything to me when I was young, and at high school I'd been obsessed with philosophy, history, art, existential questions, I'd visited museums and attended classical concerts, I'd listened to experimental jazz and found it all perfectly *straightforward*.

How could it be that a person like that, with all the essential skills required to embrace and enjoy life, should end up so damaged, so superficial, so trivial, like a tragicomic character in a Donald Duck cartoon? Why couldn't I see what I was doing, why couldn't I study myself in the same way I studied satellite photos of Iris Vilden's home, why couldn't I see the dead-end street that I'd managed to wander down, why couldn't I stand my ground?

Without any real resistance, I had trickled into a resentful ditch; drop by drop, I'd ended up in a topsy-turvy world where trivialities were important and anything genuinely significant became irrelevant.

How was the book?

The question came from behind me, and the phone fell from my hand with a clatter, I turned around.

He was standing in the doorway with carrier bags in his hands.

The manuscript, I said, correcting him. I haven't finished it yet.

Lucky for you that I've done the shopping, then, he said, holding the bags up for me to see.

I looked at him.

He was wielding a carrier bag from the off licence.

Two minutes before closing! he said. I'd completely forgotten it was Saturday.

I heaved myself out of the chair. I couldn't face a confrontation, not now, not right before Per and Hilma came over, what with his theatrical mannerisms for which she was the perfect foil.

And what kind of seafood are we going to be gorging on tonight? I asked. Seahorse and frogs' legs?

I don't think frogs really count as seafood, Kai replied, placing the bags on the worktop. Had you planned something different? I forgot to take my phone, so I couldn't ask you.

I said nothing, just started unpacking the bags.

My God, I said, are you thinking of staying for another week?

What do you mean? Kai asked, stopping and looking at me. Is there something wrong? There I was, patting myself on the back for taking care of the shopping...

Bloody hell, I mumbled, unpacking four crab shells and a pile of claws.

What? he said, sounding uncertain. I thought you liked crab?

I made a retching sound, which he overheard, and placed the shells in the fridge.

You got a text when you were out, I said, nodding at the kitchen island.

He picked up his phone, briefly glanced in my direction, and I studied him from behind the fridge door as he opened the message.

He placed his phone back down with a neutral expression.

Who was it from? I asked.

If it was all true, I'd kill her. Her first, then Kai. I'd stick hooks in her and haul her up to the ceiling of some sort of remote warehouse, hang her out to dry. The fact that she'd had the audacity to ruin things for us. Kai, too. To spoil things for us, for the boys.

Nobody, he said, and I closed the fridge door slowly.

The boys might be fine. They had a sense of humour. An incomprehensible sense of humour, certainly, but which nonetheless brought tears to my eyes whenever I observed them in secret. I checked the clock on the oven door.

I need to take a shower before they come, I said.

Don't you still have reading to do? he asked.

Bloody hell, I said. I let out a heavy sigh.

He made his way around the kitchen island and over towards me, and I stood stock-still with my arms by my sides and thought to myself that it would be worth forming an alliance with the powerful Mikkel Wexøe, I ought to call him and ask if he knew what his wife was up to, just so he could crush her on both our behalfs.

Standing in the shower, I pondered whether it was possible to survive something like this. Our marriage couldn't, not if there was any truth to my suspicions. That was lost. But me, personally. The breakdown had begun, I thought to myself as I lathered up, I could feel tumours all over me, in my armpits, my groin, my body had sprung into action, as if it had some sort of inbuilt instinct for self-destruction when a crisis occurred.

I slowly applied my makeup with trembling hands. I felt hot, a queasy feeling brought me to the verge of fainting on numerous occasions. Standing upright was a test of my strength.

Kai had opened a beer and was sitting there with his phone out as if nothing had happened when I fetched my suitcase from the hallway dressed in Iris's white dressing gown. I pulled out a clean set of underwear and a sad-looking, grey jersey dress, got myself changed as I gazed at the back of his unkempt head of hair.

She must have looked him up long ago. Found my address one day when she was bored. Found Kai's name listed at the same address. Arranged a supposedly random meeting, just for the fun of it. Seeing if you still have that same power, testing whether you can still have what you want, there's fun in that.

I had an hour left to finish reading the manuscript. I was used to skim-reading while still getting a decent grasp of things, it was something I spent much of my professional life doing.

Iris Vilden, I thought to myself. What was this all about? Was it simply intended to make me doubt myself? I had to employ Occam's razor theory: being objective, what was the simplest explanation for her ringing Kai?

She had met us in that pub, learned that I was a lawyer, asked me for advice, and as thanks for my help she had offered us the use of her cabin for the week. As thanks, but also to inspire envy on my part. Which she had partly succeeded in doing. Then she had called Kai in the hope that I would discover their communication and become jealous, a little bonus. Which, again, she had succeeded in.

But why had Kai left the room when she'd called? And why had he deleted her messages?

Because Kai knew how I felt about her. Of course.

I grabbed a beer from the fridge, sat in the chair beside Kai and made my way to page eighteen.

I had already taken her power from her once, and I'd only been thirteen at the time. I could do the same again.

Kai turned to face me and smiled, clinking his bottle against mine.

But that was too simple. Our encounter at the pub. Kai and I hadn't been into Oslo together for years, and yet on the day we finally did go, we just so happened to bump into her, of all people, completely out of the blue?

My thoughts were like a swarm of insects crawling around beneath a rock; whenever I tried to lift the rock, they slithered off and hid, I had no grasp on them at all.

I placed the pencil lengthways between my teeth and bit down as I read on about the artist, who was having dinner with her sister, the dutiful housewife.

Biting down on a pencil was something we'd learned about at a motivation workshop at work. Stick a pencil in your mouth and bite down! the workshop leader they'd brought in for the session had told us, before demonstrating herself, now your brain thinks you're smiling and your mood will improve whether you like it or not. Give it a try, she'd continued, nodding away with a pencil clamped in her jaws and a monstrous expression on her face. Try it! I bit down hard and breathed heavily through my nostrils.

Have you got a pencil in your mouth again? Kai asked, looking concerned.

What made you think I like Mahler? I asked, removing the pencil from my mouth.

Huh?

That evening at the concert hall. Why did you buy us *those* tickets in particular?

Uh, for your birthday? he replied. Why do you ask?

I don't know, I said. I prefer chamber music; I thought you knew that.

I'm hardly an expert when it comes to that kind of thing, he said. The Mahler just happened to be on at the time.

Hmm, I said, and he looked at me, and I looked back down at the manuscript. I tried to envisage the route from the concert hall to the pub, we hadn't gone the most logical way, because if he'd wanted something to eat, there were numerous places we could have chosen on the way to the station, but he had suggested we walk past the National Theatre and up Rosenkrantz' gate. And Kai had been the one to suggest that pub in particular, a pub I knew tended to host celebrations of various premiers, at least it did at one time. Kai can't have known that, he must have been told about it, I thought to myself, and I squeezed my eyes tight shut, tried to work out what it was all about, if I was losing all grasp on reality, losing myself in conspiracy theories.

All those times he'd been away for work over the past two years, all those nights, had he been *here* all along, with her? While I sat alone, shut up at home with the boys?

What did Iris have to say? I asked, breezily.

Iris?

Yes, in her text?

Nothing, he said. I told her I'd finished work on the jetty and she sent me a thumbs-up.

He brought his bottle to his lips nonchalantly, his Adam's apple moved upwards, he swallowed.

So, you've been deleting your texts as you go, then, I said, my eyes on the manuscript.

He looked at me.

Have you been going through my phone?

What? Surely you've got nothing to hide?

Karin, what is this? he said, placing the bottle down on the table.

Good question, what *is* this? I replied. What exactly is going on?

Nothing! he shouted. What did you think was going on? Did you think there was something happening between us?

Well, I don't know, I replied. Is there?

He gazed at me, wide-eyed.

Have you lost your mind? he said.

Maybe, I said. What do you think?

What do I think? I think you're obsessed with the woman, Kai said. I think you're jealous, and...

And what? I asked calmly.

Is your life any worse just because Iris's is good? he asked.

I shrugged, forced a modest smile.

Yes, or no?

Yes, I replied.

Yes? Really? he said. Do you realise what you're saying? You've got two lovely boys, a good job, a house, you've got me...

A house covered in horrible textured wallpaper, I said, and he looked at me, open-mouthed.

This isn't you, he said eventually, and I said nothing, just rolled my eyes.

How long have you known her? I asked him, turning to look him in the eye.

What? he asked, and he stood up, as if repulsed, and his reaction was so unlike him that I knew there was something there. I swallowed the lump in my throat.

How long had you been planning our meeting that evening? I asked him calmly, looking straight at him.

I don't know what you're talking about! he cried, bringing his hands to his head. Can you hear yourself? But before I could say a word, he hushed me, holding my gaze as he crept backwards towards the kitchen window and cautiously peeped outside.

It's them, he whispered.

They're way too early, I hissed back, looking at the clock. I haven't even read a sixth of this thing!

He gestured that he wasn't sure what to do, and so I gathered the manuscript into a pile, just as I heard a knock at the door.

I stood up, lifted the chair cushion and shoved the manuscript underneath it, and Per Sinding poked his head around the door.

Buona sera! he said, stepping inside and casually placing a Brunello on the kitchen island with the discreet charm of the bourgeoisie. He looked at Kai and then at me, then the partially unpacked food on the worktop, and he stopped.

Are we early?

No, no, we're just running a little behind, Kai said. Come on in.

Head outside and sit down, I said.

Is it me, or are you two giving us mixed signals? Per said, and Hilma Ekhult slipped in behind him, silent, as if on paws.

Welcome, I said, pressing my lips together in something

resembling a smile, and Hilma pressed her lips together back at me.

I don't suppose a little look around would be out of the question? Per said, looking at Kai and then back at me.

Of course, Kai said. Knock yourselves out.

Very modern, Per said, taking a few steps into the living room. It's hardly a cabin at all. Do you call it a cabin?

We do, Kai said.

It's a summer house, I said.

A summer house, Kai repeated, thoughtfully.

May we...? Hilma said, walking in the direction of the other wing, and I held my breath and slowly released it.

Of course, Kai said, just along here is the bedroom, the guest bedroom, the bathroom, and a small office.

He followed them and Per stopped all of a sudden.

And who do we have here?

Kai fell silent and turned to face me slowly, and his face collapsed.

What's that? I asked, and I moved in their direction before stopping in my tracks.

Per Sinding was standing in front of the portrait of the Vilden-Wexøe family.

That's my brother and his wife, I said quickly, casting a furious glance in Kai's direction, as if he had some special responsibility for removing the picture of Iris and her family.

Aha, Per said. He turned to look at Hilma.

There's something familiar about them, don't you think? he said, and she cocked her head to one side in response.

Not surprising really, I said. We share this place with them.

It'd be a waste to keep it all to ourselves, Kai added, keen to play along, because quite unexpectedly I had solved the problem facing us both, namely the prospect of Per wandering past at a later date and finding a completely different family in situ.

They're coming next week, I said. But they're not so keen on having visitors, I'm afraid.

We promise to keep our distance, Per said.

Shall we sit outside? I asked, trying once again to move proceedings outdoors, and their little tour came to an end as they all turned around.

Per and Hilma glanced at one another and obediently made their way outside, where they took a seat.

Your brother? Kai said when we were alone once again, tapping his temple with one finger. Quick thinking, Karin.

Thank you, I said.

I made my way over to the fridge and pulled out one of the bottles he had bought, I was surprised to see it was the same Alta Langa I usually bought to go with crab, Kai must have remembered.

I opened the bottle with a controlled *pfff*, filled a glass and drank half of it in one gulp.

It didn't make any sense. Why would she invite me, us, out here? Why would she risk me finding out? Unless she *wanted* me to find out. Of course.

But Kai, I thought, he wouldn't want that, would he?

I knew that I couldn't afford to lose him. Not for financial or practical reasons, and not because it would mean finding somewhere else to live, even though that was also true, but because losing him would mean losing everything. Everything I had, everything in my life, it was all so intricately connected to him. 'I don't know who I am without him', I'd heard people say that, but I was all too well aware of who I was without Kai.

I finished my glass and refilled it.

I lifted my gaze as Kai reappeared in the doorway.

Are you coming? he asked.

I held his gaze as I drank, another half-glass down the hatch, he looked at me nervously.

Is everything OK, Karin?

I'm coming, I said.

I sat down on the bench beside Per, and Kai emerged with the dressed crab and claws arranged on a large plate with the ubiquitous mayonnaise, bread and lemon.

Help yourselves, Kai said, passing the dish to Per, who first served Hilma, then himself, then passed the plate to me.

I felt that Hilma was sending small, subtle glances in my direction, stopping only when I looked over at her. I assumed that she was nervously scrutinising me to try to decipher what I thought about her work.

So, I looked into investing in timber earlier today, Per said to Kai. Didn't look all that promising. That was a joke, I assume?

That *was* a joke, yes, Kai said quickly.

Very funny, Per said, holding his gaze, bringing his fork to his mouth.

Kai helped himself without looking up, while Hilma chewed on her crab, her jaw barely moving, and Per embarked on a monologue about childhood summers in east Telemark, his large family and his relationship with his siblings.

And how about you, Hilma said out of the blue, looking up at us, do you have children?

Two, I said. Two boys, aged seven and nine.

That sounds lively, Per said cheerfully.

He was assuming that two boys of that age must be a couple of tearaways, oh hardy-har, can you imagine! Two little idiots compared to their suntanned, long-legged daughter with her perfectly straight, white teeth, well on her way to becoming an experienced neurosurgeon or the youngest ever professor of psychology at some prestigious US college or a UN-delegate in a few short years.

They take care of themselves, really, I said. The eldest is obsessed with his piano. He plays that thing until he's on the brink of passing out. The seven-year-old loves chess and football, it keeps him busy all day long. We hardly see them, do we? I said, looking at Kai.

It's hard to believe they're ours, really, Kai said.

And you don't get tired of all this piano playing? Per asked.

It's an electronic keyboard, I said quickly, he wears his headphones. We can only hear the pedals.

That sounds nice, Hilma said, looking at Per.

I couldn't face the prospect of asking them about their daughter, couldn't abide the idea of having to hear about her various merits and distinctions, Person of the Year.

And what about your daughter? Kai asked, clearly growing uncomfortable at the lies I'd told about our sons. What's she up to these days? She's twenty, isn't she?

Twenty, yes, Hilma said.

And she's a student, is she? Kai asked.

No, she... Hilma began, and she stopped.

She still lives at home, I think I mentioned that yesterday, Per said, looking over at Hilma. She closed her eyes and gave a curt nod.

Unfortunately, like so many others, she suffers with ME.

Oh no, Kai said, setting down his cutlery.

That's why we're still in Stockholm, Hilma said. A move wouldn't be good for her.

We were only intending on staying over there for a few years, Per said. But it's been almost eight now.

Has she been ill for long? Kai asked.

It must be, what, five, six years since she became really ill? Per said, looking inquiringly at Hilma.

Six, Hilma said. She was only fourteen at the time.

I'm sorry to hear that, I said.

It's probably the reason things haven't gone very smoothly for us on the work front over these past few years, Per said. We've had a lot on our plate.

Poor girl, I said, but amidst the instinctive saccharine *schadenfreude* I felt – they had their struggles in life too, ill health, money problems, why on earth did that bring me any sort of joy? – I also felt a warmth spread through me that at least partially suppressed my feelings of inferiority and admiration, not to mention the constant fear I had of being exposed as a liar: I felt genuinely sorry for them. I swelled with unexpected and sincere emotion, there were tears in my eyes, and immediately I felt the pounding of my guilty conscience for not having read her manuscript.

They'd shown such confidence in us, and all on spurious grounds, and yes – I had betrayed them. But couldn't I just tell them I needed more time? That I hadn't had the time to finish reading it? But it was Saturday, we were leaving tomorrow, I couldn't spin this out any longer. I could just tell her that I loved it, plead with her to send it back to the publishing house, insist on a new editor, threaten to move to a different publisher. They ought to be made aware of the difficult situation with her daughter, surely they should be doing anything in their power to help and support their most important author?

Kai emerged with a second bottle of wine to go with the crab, he topped up our glasses and joined in the conversation, which was predominantly steered by Per.

When did they finish work on this place? Per asked suddenly, turning to look at Kai, and I felt my stomach drop.

This place? Spring, the year before last, Kai replied calmly.

Fairly recently, then, Per said. And there was something here before that, was there?

A dilapidated old shack built in the 1950s, Kai said.

I see, was it in the family?

No, no, Kai said, we bought the old place, tore it down and built this instead.

Aha, Per said. And the cladding...

Ore-pine, Kai said.

Mmm, Per said, bringing his glass to his lips.

Is this an interview? Hilma asked, looking at him with her eyebrow raised.

No, no, Per said. I'm just interested. I may have mentioned before that we want to add a little guest annex to our own cabin, but they refused us permission. But here – I don't imagine that the old cabin looked anything like this?

Well, Kai said, it was actually two small cabins side-by-side at a similar angle, so the base is virtually identical.

You must remember it, Per, Hilma said, sounding irritated, you must remember what the old cabins looked like? We've passed by in the boat more times than I can remember.

Of course, Per said. My point is simply that it's very different in appearance from what was here before it.

As I said, Kai continued, the foundations are the same, and all our planning applications went through without issue.

Per had nothing to say in response. He took another sip of his drink.

Nobody was eating any longer. There was still crab left on the plate. I nudged it in Hilma's direction, who automatically raised a palm.

Per discreetly studied the label on the bottle. He wanted to remember it. Kai sipped his beer straight from the bottle. I got up and cleared the table, stacked everything on a tray and took it into the kitchen.

I opened the red wine Per had placed on the kitchen island, found a glass and filled it, leaned on the kitchen worktop and brought the glass to my lips. I drank it with a sigh. His small talk outside was tireless. He was a confusing individual, preoccupied with making an impression, yet equally preoccupied with demonstrating that we were making no impression on him.

The door opened, and I turned around. It was him.

There were rumours of a toilet around here somewhere...

Just there, I said, first on the left.

He walked past me and into the other half of the cabin. I arranged the plates in the dishwasher and turned it on, wiped the bench, grabbed some cups.

Can I help with anything? I heard a voice ask behind me, and I turned around to find Per looking at me.

Thanks, everything's under control here, I said.

That's an Americanism, Per said. *Everything's under control.*

That's true, I said, brushing his comment off.

It's nice stuff, isn't it? Per said, nodding at the bottle he'd brought with him.

Yes, not bad for one of the more affordable brunellos, I said, and I found him a clean glass, which he accepted with mild irritation.

I poured him a glass and we toasted with a gentle clink. Neither of us spoke. He swallowed before taking a deep breath in through his nostrils and exhaling with a slight groan. I could hear Kai outside, attempting to make conversation with Hilma.

Lovely, Per murmured.

Indeed.

So, he said, leaning in and lowering his voice. Have you read it?

I ... have, yes, I said, with a slow and mysterious nod.

And? he said.

Yes, I said. I liked it very much. It's good.

'Good'?

I lowered my voice and leaned in closer.

It's fantastic.

He closed his eyes and let out a brief sigh.

You're sure? he said, and for a moment he looked as if he might burst into tears.

There now, I said, isn't that good news?

He opened his eyes and gazed at me with the look of a dog begging for scraps.

Could you tell her, do you think? Do you think you might be able to convince her? She listens to you.

I felt some kindness towards him. His arrogant, extroverted behaviour, knowingly making a fool of himself to distract from Hilma's stand-offish behaviour. His theatricality was like a shield for her, and within that there was a declaration of love. He knew and accepted that she was more important than him.

I'll do what I can. You head on outside and I'll be right out with the coffee.

He stopped at the door and mouthed a 'thank you' at me before turning around and going outside.

It was half past eight. The sun had gone down a while ago and had been replaced by a cool breeze. Hilma had arranged a lavender, lightweight-wool jacket over her shoulders like a cape.

You were hoping to have a word with Hilma, weren't you, Karin? Per said once I'd set down the coffee cups.

Hilma looked at Per in surprise, who stood up.

How about it then, Kai? he said. Fancy a few casts?

Um, why not? Kai replied. He took two cups from the tray and made his way towards Per. Hilma watched them go, looking unsure, and then we were alone once again.

Well now, I said, sitting opposite her, and Hilma pressed her lips together in her usual way, looking slightly uneasy without making eye contact. She brought the cup to her lips and took a cautious sip, her top lip protruding. I popped two chocolates in my mouth to give myself the energy boost I needed to go through her manuscript with her, gulped down my coffee.

Well, I've read it, I said gently once I'd swallowed, and she turned her tiny head to look at me.

Read what? she asked.

The manuscript. I've read it.

What manuscript? she asked.

I looked at her and she looked at me, her brow furrowed.

Your manuscript. The one that Per...

That Per what?

Oh, I see, I muttered quietly. He's given it to me without your knowledge.

Per gave you a copy of my manuscript? she said slowly.

He told me you'd asked him to. I'm as surprised as you are about all this.

She leaned back in her chair, furious or simply stunned, I couldn't quite tell.

I'm sorry...

And you've read it, she said.

This was it, my opportunity to admit that I *hadn't* actually read it after all, but I didn't take it.

I have, I confirmed.

She took a deep breath, as if to control herself, then grabbed her cup of coffee once again and took another sip.

The damage is done, then, she said eventually, looking straight at me with her lucid, light-grey eyes. I'd only ask that you forget about it. It's not to be published, at any rate.

Forget about it?

I printed it out yesterday evening, she said. Started reading it. Then threw it away.

You can't just dismiss it like that, I said. It's good!

She smiled bitterly, as if my words had revealed how much reading I did in my day-to-day life, or what I chose to read, perhaps, but she said nothing.

I do my fair share of reading, as I mentioned yesterday, I said. And I really liked the way you—

She cut me off with a wave of her hand.

Let's not discuss it, she said.

Well, that's a shame, I said. You won't see any progress with that approach.

I drank the rest of my coffee in one fell swoop.

She cocked her head to one side and narrowed her eyes antagonistically.

Perhaps you think you've already written everything you're meant to write? I said. By the age of, what, fifty-something?

Fifty-five, she said.

That's that, then, I said. The world will never know the work you might otherwise have written, the significance that work—

Significance, she repeated, interrupting me mid-flow, and let out a snort.

I poured myself some more wine, held the bottle in her direction, she nodded. I topped up her glass with a generous glug and Hilma grasped the stem and drank.

No, no, I said. Well, that's a real shame. Very few people write like you do. Naked plot, no lingering on descriptions or passing of moral judgement, sober use of language, and yet so captivating.

She raised an eyebrow slightly, as I'd expected she would, curious as to where this level of precision had come from, but without revealing the slightest hint of pleasure upon hearing my words of praise.

Aha, she said, quite simply.

You need to end your working relationship with your editor. The fact that he's failed to help you through this, that he's failed to finish this book with you, that's a serious matter.

And what exactly did you like about it? she asked instead, out of the blue, but before I was able to open my mouth to reply, she batted her own question away with a flourish.

As I said, I replied. Loading such snappy sentences with that degree of emotional impact, building that sort of smouldering...

But? Hilma Ekhult said.

There is no but, I replied.

There's a but.

No.

What did you make of the ending? she asked, putting down her glass and looking straight at me.

The ending?

Yes.

The ending felt – slightly curbed, perhaps? I guessed.

She let out a sharp, uncomfortable cackle.

To put it mildly, she said.

But that can be changed, I said. It wouldn't take much.

I had to extricate myself from it, the sooner, the better.

The ending, I began, surely it has to provide some sort of response to the protagonist's obvious issue?

Which is? Hilma replied, looking at me very calmly.

She doubts her own artistic worth, I said. She creates work that everyone will like. It says nothing of significance, but it's aesthetically pleasing, modern art that threatens nobody.

Quite, Hilma said, her ears pricked up like an animal on high alert, and emboldened by her response I carried on, continuing to make a stab at the protagonist's real issue.

She doubts her art because she doubts herself. She produces work without any real significance because she feels that she is an insignificant person at risk of being exposed at any given moment.

To think, I've missed that all along, she said with a bitter smile.

I stopped.

Missed what?

The fact that it's a self-portrait. How could I have failed to see it all this time?

I opened my mouth to speak, but she interrupted me.

No, she said. You're right. It doesn't mean anything. None of it means anything.

What? I replied.

Thank you, she said. Thank you for your honesty. I appreciate it. Not many people in this world are really, *truly* honest.

She grabbed her handbag, as if she were making to leave, taking her crushed self-confidence with her.

What did I say? I asked. Whatever it was, I didn't mean it like that. I'm not a good reader after all, I'm sure I've completely misunderstood your protagonist.

She placed her handbag in her lap and turned to look at me.

No, you haven't misunderstood a thing, she said.

I took a deep breath.

I haven't read it! I exclaimed. I didn't finish it, I only got to page eighteen! I couldn't get hold of Kai, I thought he'd had an accident out at sea, and I...

She looked at me and raised an eyebrow.

That doesn't matter, you're right all the same. I write appealing page-turners for people with good taste and money to burn.

No, I said. You're one of— I stopped myself mid-sentence. Well, so what? If they're good books?

She sighed in a condescending manner.

The way you portray nature, I said, I had to get her off this track, it reminded me of the landscape around here. Is this where you work?

I don't work, she said.

But you were here when you wrote this, weren't you?

A week here and there, sure. I don't get the chance to spend very long out here.

Your daughter? I said.

Yes, she replied. She gets anxious.

You can't come out here by yourself? I asked. You and Per can't take it in turns?

It's not where I'm sitting that's the problem, she said. The problem is that it's hard for me to think about anything else when she's unwell.

I understood that.

She fell silent once again.

And she can't come out here with you? I asked. If it's here you like to work?

She looked at me, and her pale-grey eyes seemed to darken.

There have been periods of time when she's been completely bed-bound, she said. She hasn't even been able to turn over without help. She hasn't been able to sit up, or to speak. I've had to feed her with a spoon.

I swallowed.

She's not like that now, but the idea that it might happen again? Any kind of travel is too much of a risk.

But you mentioned an annexe, I said. Was that with her in mind? The possibility that she might come out here with you?

It was something she expressed an interest in during one of her good spells. That was a long time ago now. A simple little place to call her own.

Aha, I said. Might there be something in that idea?

We've already asked and been turned down.

Turned down? What do you mean?

Planning permission, she hissed impatiently.

You need to seek permission to demolish your outhouse, I said. Then build on the existing foundations. A bedroom, a small bathroom and a little living room.

Yes, she said, gazing into the distance. But I'm sure the answer would be the same. And moving Simone out here and back again, it just wouldn't work.

What if you were all to live out here permanently? I suggested.

She gave a resigned smile.

It's not impossible, I said, keenly.

Per has already looked into it. This whole area is reserved for holiday homes.

Well, sure, but you can always apply for an exemption, I said.

She gave a cold, curt chuckle.

We can't even get permission to build a small annexe.

Apply for a change of use.

It's ironic, isn't it? Two authors left helpless when it comes to writing a simple application, she remarked dryly, and I racked my brains to work out if she was using the word 'ironic' correctly.

But there was a fire in her eyes. She and Per and Simone, here all year round, living in their own little house surrounded by fresh, sea air.

But you don't need to *write* an application, I said, chuckling stoically, picturing them helplessly flapping around one another, tearing their hair out as they tried to add an attachment to an email.

Wait here, I said, and I got up and went inside, returning with my iPad.

Look at this, I said, and I opened the county council's website and clicked my way through its complicated infrastructure. There was nothing difficult about this for me.

This is the county council website, right? Watch this. Here's the menu. Click on Planning, Building and Property,

OK? Then click on this – Build, Demolish, Alter, and then select Apply, and there you have it.

A form? she said.

You might have to pay a higher rate of tax to live here year-round, I said, clicking on the link. But that would be worth it, surely?

She looked as if she'd stopped breathing, sitting there and watching me at work, craning her smooth neck to see what I was doing.

Change of Use, I mumbled, so you're the registered owner, the building is on your land, it's a detached structure, to be converted from a second home to a primary residence – there you go.

I felt like a seventeen-year-old hacker breaking into the servers of a hostile foreign nation.

And this is where you submit, I said, showing her the submission page. It's very simple.

And you really think...?

I don't see why not, I replied. You've got running water and electricity and access, haven't you? All the technicalities are already in place.

She stared at the screen, said nothing.

You could submit it here and now, if you wanted to. You just need to fill in the address. You're Kilodden, too, aren't you?

That's right, she said, though I'm not quite sure which number we are...

I opened the map on my iPad and the blue dot located us immediately. I moved the map to the west side of the headland and located her cabin. Could it be number twelve? I asked, holding the iPad up for her to see.

That sounds right, she said keenly, and her eyes seemed to glow. It wasn't a bogus literary consultant she needed; it was a Nittedal County Council consultant.

I'm sure that must be right, I said, we're Kilodden eighteen.

I switched to aerial view, and the blue dot returned to the roof of our cabin, the two rectangles converging to form one building. My gaze fell on a tiny orange rectangle at the end of the gravel track, in the exact location where our van was parked at this very moment in time.

Weird, I thought to myself, zooming in, is this map in real time or something, a live image beamed from a satellite?

So? Hilma said, and I looked at her.

What?

Are you going to send it? she asked.

I can do, I said, clearing my throat, do you want me to? Or do you want to speak to Per first?

I grabbed my glass of water and drank, tried taking deep breaths, filled my glass once again.

Speak to Per? she replied. Why would I do that? I'm a feminist, aren't I?

She let out a bright, high-pitched giggle and gave me a cheerful, knowing look, but I maintained a neutral expression.

There, I said. That's all sent. Don't expect to hear back for a few weeks, though.

Gracious, she said. I hadn't expected that from you.

She brought a hand to her heart, took a deep breath and looked at me, revitalised.

I let her smile linger between us and she looked at me for a moment before getting up.

Excuse me, she said. I just need to use...

Once she had gone inside, I opened the aerial view on the map once again, zoomed in on the cabin. It must have been taken in the early autumn, the grass was a faint shade of yellowish-brown, not the lush, verdant green of spring. The greyish sea was pale down by the old jetty. And at the end of the gravel track: there was no mistaking it, it was an orange van.

I closed my eyes, brought my hands to my face and let out a silent chuckle. So it was true.

It must have been going on for six months, at least. Since the autumn. Longer, probably.

The concert, those *terrible* seats, and still I had been so delighted. It had all been a set-up. The meeting in the pub had been arranged. He had acted as if he had no idea who she was, and all as part of what, some sort of hilarious game? I didn't understand it, was it part of a bigger plan to belittle me, meeting right in front of me like that, had I stood there, thick as two short planks, listing arguments she could use in some made-up meeting with the theatre?

Is the seminar almost over? a voice asked, and I jumped.

Per came up behind me as Kai made his way over to the wall of the cabin and fetched an armful of birch logs from the woodstore.

Where is she? Per asked, suspicious, or nervous, perhaps, what might I have done with her?

She's in the loo, I said, closing the cover on the iPad. Kai carried the wood to the fire pit, tore strips of birch bark from the logs and stacked them up.

So, how did it go? Per whispered.

Well, I think, I told him absent-mindedly, and he grasped my shoulders and gave me an appreciative shake without saying a word.

There you are, Hilma said as she emerged from the cabin and slowly made her way towards Per.

I can't believe you gave her that manuscript... she said, and she pointed a finger firmly against his chest. Per held his palms up to her and stepped back, taking a seat on the bench next to me.

Kai had got the fire going, the flames rippled against the pale-yellow sky.

As luck would have it, Karin didn't have a chance to read it, she said, and Per turned to look at me, opening his mouth as if to speak.

Kai? Another drink? I asked.

Hilma sat down opposite me, looking at me with a secretive twinkle in her eye.

Well? Shall we tell them? she asked, and Per looked at her.

What's all this? he asked.

Karin thinks there's a good chance we can live out here full-time.

Per opened his mouth in surprise and looked at me.

I can't make any guarantees, I said. But I can't imagine the council would have any objections to you making this your permanent residence.

He looked at Hilma.

What do you mean?

We can move out here, all three of us, she said, and her face broke into a smile.

Probably, I chipped in.

The application's already been sent.

Per sat back with his mouth open, looking at Hilma and then at me.

So, you two were having a planning meeting, were you? he said. This is quite something.

It's what we've dreamed about, Hilma said. Just think what this could mean for Simone, away from all the noise and pollution.

Uh huh? Per said, looking at me. And you helped make this a reality, did you?

I can't make any promises, I said. But I think there's a good chance your application will be approved.

Now it's just a case of thinking about the annexe, Hilma said, looking at Per. Karin says we ought to tear down the outhouse and seek planning permission to build on its foundations, isn't that right, Karin? Is it just one form for that too?

Woah woah woah now, Per said. Let's just take a moment here.

Do we need to use a particular architectural firm? Hilma asked.

Pardon?

Who designed this cabin for you?

Snøhetta, I replied.

It *was* Snøhetta! Hilma said, giving Per a triumphant look. I told you so.

I didn't think Snøhetta were still very in these days, he replied.

Who was it at Snøhetta, do you remember? Hilma asked.

This might all be moving a little fast, I said. This is a very different sort of...

The annexe could be very different in style to the rest of the cabin, something a bit more modern, simple but functional, for Simone, Hilma said.

Per looked at me expectantly.

We just need a name, Hilma said.

She... I said, and I felt the need to swallow, but forced myself to refrain. Throughout my life I'd always remembered something I'd once read in a book about lying, about how bad people are at exposing liars. People generally assume that other people are telling the truth. We trust people who appear to be honest and who tell the truth. We trust people who appear to be honest and who tell lies. We trust those who appear to be dishonest and who speak the truth. Only those who appear dishonest *and* who tell lies can be exposed as the liars they are.

Up until this point in time, I had lied while appearing to be honest. Now I had started to grow weary. I couldn't keep it up forever.

Gosh, who was it again, I said vaguely, turning to look at Kai, who stepped out of the cabin empty-handed.

Kai, can you remember? The name of our architect?

Hmm, afraid not, Kai said. You were the one in touch with her.

Maybe you still have her number, Hilma suggested.

Silence fell between us, and all that could be heard was the crackling of burning wood.

I'd rather not say, I said.

The pair of them looked at me with bated breath.

Relax, Per said. We're not planning on *copying* your cabin.

You'd rather not say? Hilma said.

She does a lot of work with environmentally-friendly concrete, Kai said.

But I'm sure you two must know your fair share of architects? I said.

Why won't you tell us? Hilma said.

It's the same kind of cement that the ancient Romans used, Kai told Per, turning to look at me. What's it called, again, that Roman cement?

I said nothing. Hilma looked straight at me, waiting.

I relaxed, completely and utterly, let it all go.

We haven't been completely honest with you, I said, looking at Hilma.

No? she said.

We... I began, and I had to swallow after all, far too loudly. I looked at Kai, who sat there frozen, I felt as if all the many lies I'd stacked on top of one another began to tumble down around me, the wall was crumbling.

I'm not ... this isn't actually...

Pozzolan! Kai cried. Sand, slaked lime and volcanic ash. That's it, the Roman cement I was talking about.

What were you going to say? Hilma asked, her eyes on me.

We're not— I began, but Kai interrupted me once again.

The height of the roof, he said quickly, and Hilma and Per both turned to look at him.

It's sixty-eight centimetres higher than it should be, he said.

The roof...? Hilma said.

The roof, Kai repeated. This building is taller than is strictly permitted.

Aha! Per said. All is revealed.

I altered the drawings before I handed them over to our builder, Kai said. The architect doesn't know. We'd rather she didn't...

Well, well, well, it's about time we had some dirt on you, Per said, chuckling.

Ignore him, Hilma said.

Imagine if the council found out, Per said.

Yes, said Kai, imagine, and he looked at me quickly, an odd expression on his face. We'd have to tear the whole place down.

Tear it down? Hilma repeated, looking sceptical.

Of course, Per said. They're ruthless about that sort of thing around here.

Well, we're not worried about any of that, Hilma said, brushing off his comment with the wave of a hand.

No? Kai said. I was sure that you'd noticed.

It was only thanks to the dusk that the thudding of my pulse in my neck wasn't visible for all to see.

Well, we've unburdened ourselves, at the very least, Kai said.

The aim of any artistic endeavour, Per said. To peel away as many layers of untruth as possible.

Kai? I said. Shall we open another bottle?

I think we're all out, he said.

Out? I said. Already?

I only bought the two.

I let out a groan.

Don't you have a wine cellar? Per asked.

We don't even have a *cellar* cellar, Kai replied.

Where on earth do you store your potatoes? Per asked, and Kai gave a wan smile.

Well, it's clear we need more wine, Per said. This is when the party really gets started.

Sorry, Kai said. It's all gone.

Then we'll take the boat over to ours and fetch a few bottles, Per said.

Kai looked at me. I shook my head subtly.

Yes? Per said. Super!

I'll join you, Hilma said quickly.

You're not turning in for the night, are you? I asked.

Oh no, I just don't want to leave it to Per to select the wine, who knows what he'll come back with, she said.

Kai, will you come with me?

Sure? he replied, looking at Per.

The two of them made their way down the steps towards the water like the mismatched pair they were, Kai somewhat reluctant and Hilma looking regal. I realised this was the last I would be seeing of her, and relief washed over me.

When they were out of sight I turned to look at Per. He was leaning back and staring into the distance.

So, you didn't read it, then, he said flatly.

You gave it to me without Hilma's knowledge, I replied.

It was lying in the waste-paper basket in her office, he said. You must have said something yesterday that made her want to print it out and take another look.

He reached for his packet of cigarettes and pulled one out, then lit it with the long lighter used to get the fire going.

Fantastic, you said, he remarked. But you hadn't even read it. Was it too much trouble?

I just didn't have the... I began, then stopped in my tracks. I read the first eighteen pages. They were good. But work has been hectic lately. There's a lot going on, I can't say any more than that, it's a stock-market matter, a sensitive one.

He blew the smoke out through his nose and tilted his head back.

I thought there was something about you, something ... spirited, he said. Hilma, you know, she's surrounded by yes-men. Her publisher, her readers, even her critics, they heap praise upon her, it never stops. It's had the opposite effect to what was intended, though, it's only made her all the more critical of herself, because she knows that none of the feedback she's getting is completely honest. But to hear something from someone on the outside, someone like you, an individual working in a different field entirely, someone with a fresh perspective and without that sense of reverence...

He turned to look at me.

I thought you might have something of value to offer.

It's inside, I said, I can still read it, if you really think...

He shook his head.

She won't be doing any more writing, he said. Not now she thinks she's moving out here, building Simone her own little Snøhetta cabin, who knows what other desperate measures she'll find to prolong this period of writer's block.

Don't you think a change might do some good? I asked.

He smirked.

Silence fell between us, leaving only the crackle of the birch on the fire, the swell of the water, the odd screech of a gull overhead. It had grown noticeably cooler. Per breathed in and out slowly, calmly.

I trusted you, he said.

I tried to force my breath down into my gut, but it was lodged in my chest, my shoulders ached.

I felt the darkness creep over me. What was there to

return home to after all this? The entire summer lay ahead of us, but all I could see was a complex, solid-grey silence separating Kai and me, confrontations, anxious boys.

I took the cigarette out of Per's hand, popped it between my lips and took a deep drag on it, he said nothing.

A cold fury swept over me as I reflected on the way in which Kai had jeopardised everything, as if the life we had wasn't the slightest bit important, as if it wasn't worth anything when it came down to it.

I exhaled and put the cigarette out on the stone table top.

I knew he had been watching me. There had been brief moments every so often, his eyes had lingered on me, he thought I hadn't noticed. The kind of thing Kai didn't pick up on, it would simply never have occurred to him.

Well now, Per said, filling the silence, and at that moment I placed my hand on his thigh, nonchalant, as if it were nothing, without saying a word; a cold quiver moved through me.

Now, now, Karin, he said, sounding almost disappointed, and he took my wrist between his thumb and index finger and calmly moved my hand away. What's wrong?

Kai's been unfaithful.

He turned to look at me.

That's why I didn't get to finish reading the manuscript, we were arguing...

Are you sure? he said, his voice low, brow furrowed.

Yes.

He sighed quietly.

You know, Hilma and I have had our hurdles to overcome, too, he said. It doesn't have to be the end of the world.

This wasn't just a one-off incident, I said. It's been going on for a long time. It's been planned.

Things changed for us when Simone fell ill, he continued, not listening to what I was saying. Since then, we've been united in all things at all times. Neither of us has had any cause to doubt the other.

I thought about the house. We wouldn't be able to keep it. The boys were so happy there, and it was within walking distance of their school, their friends. Kai's workshop was there.

Children are more important than anything, Per said.

I said nothing. I'd wanted so badly for them to be as reliable as Kai. To inherit his effortless, instinctive self-confidence. Instead, I often saw my own flaws when I looked at them.

Things might work themselves out, Per said.

They don't play chess and piano, I said. They play video games.

Hilma and I, we go to couples therapy together, he said.

Not because there's a problem, but it helps, it's like a safety valve.

Our eldest puts on a baby voice whenever he feels nervous, I said.

He looked at me.

Sorry, I said. I know that's nothing compared with...

He didn't reply.

Maybe we could figure something out that would mean the boys could always be in the house, I thought to myself, with Kai and I living one week on, one week off alongside them, and in a small flat somewhere the rest of the time. Then they'd be spared the hassle of moving around all the time, at least, shunted back and forth between an unfaithful father and a depressed mother.

He told me I could take him for granted! I said.

I'm going to need that manuscript back, Per said. It mustn't fall into the wrong hands.

Of course, I said, getting up.

I left him and made my way back inside, he watched me go.

I walked through the dark living room and lifted the cushion, gathered the papers from underneath it and looked around for the folder, finding it on the kitchen worktop by the coffee machine.

I could see the fire through the kitchen window, his face,

he sat motionless on the bench, leaning back, the light of the flames illuminating his features, his arrogant aquiline nose.

I needed something stronger.

I pushed the freezer drawer with my foot, but it was the wrong one, there were only cloth napkins inside, all neatly folded beside a stack of books. Who keeps books in a kitchen drawer? I wondered, as I went to push it back in, but I stopped when I spotted the title of the book on the top of the pile. The cover was black with bronze lettering: *Attica*.

Underneath, in smaller letters: *Per Sinding*, and I stopped breathing. Not that strange, really, I thought to myself, a little agitated, they know he's their neighbour, they're curious about him. I bent down and picked up the book, opened it and turned to the title page, and there it was, in fountain pen, cursive handwriting in dark-blue ink:

> *August 2021*
> *To Iris and Mikkel,*
> *With thanks for all the wonderful summer*
> *evenings we've spent together.*
> *Per*

A pounding sensation in my head, a crackling, a rushing in my ears like the swell of the waves, spots danced around in front of my eyes as the blood rushed out of my head.

I sank down onto the floor, my head between my knees, did my best to breathe deeply and calmly.

He'd known all along.

From the moment he'd come here that first evening.

He'd played along with such glee; whatever next? Studied us with a wry smile all the while, look at the two idiots pretending to be someone else, they actually thought they'd pulled it off, *believed* that they were believable.

I squeezed my eyes tight shut as I heard the echo of everything I'd said over the past few days.

Did he know my name, my real name, what I did, had he held back his laughter for days on end?

And what about Hilma, did she know? Was she in on it?

I placed my hands on the floor, my fingers were cold and white. I got to my feet, wobbling slightly, reached out and grabbed the kitchen worktop and looked out, he was still motionless out there in the darkness.

Did he know Iris well enough to tell her about all this

by the fire one night, the pair of them cackling in disbelief?

I had no feeling in my feet, but I set one in front of the other until I reached the door; I stepped outside and he looked up. I stopped.

Here, I said, handing him the manuscript and slowly sitting down opposite him.

Everything alright? he asked.

I said nothing.

You're very pale.

So you've known all along? I said. From the moment you came over here that evening?

Known what? he asked, leaning in.

That I... I said, but I couldn't go on.

He looked at me, waiting.

You know Iris, I said flatly.

He sat back.

Of course I know Iris, he said. We're neighbours.

I took a deep breath in, wanted to laugh out loud, but it got caught in my throat.

We're hardly in regular contact, but we share the odd bottle of wine now and again.

And Hilma?

He gave me a resigned look.

You know Hilma. Not the world's most sociable individual.

Don't say anything to her. Please. We're leaving tomorrow. You'll never see us again.

I know, he said.

I closed my eyes.

Exciting stuff, I must say, he said. Having the opportunity to study two – well, what would you call yourselves exactly, impersonators? – at such close quarters.

I was about to respond when he stopped me.

You know, I came over that evening to apologise, he said. For the way I'd spoken to you.

I felt a thudding in my gut.

But after that, I just had to call Iris and ask her. I hadn't heard anything about them selling up.

You called Iris, I said, my voice was no longer my own, it sounded almost guttural. Did you tell her...?

But she was able to ease any concerns I had, as you well know. She had bumped into a skilled carpenter she knew, she said. Who happened to be married to a childhood friend of hers – that's you, apparently. Iris certainly knows how to take advantage of people. A free jetty in exchange for a week's holiday here in the murky shadows of 'the solar eclipse', as we like to call it? I'm not sure who got the better end of the deal.

The flames rippled silently in the fire pit, in the process of dying out.

I stared into the distance, my face and mouth frozen, my eyes swollen.

Well, Per said, standing up. I think we'd best call it a night. He turned to look at me.

It's been interesting getting to know you, Karin. I hope things work themselves out between you and Kai.

So Kai didn't... I whispered as he left, making his way over the grass and up the smooth, coastal rock, until I could see only his shoulders, then the back of his head, then nothing at all against the blue, June night sky.

I sat there until the fire went out. I was freezing. It was silent all around, besides the slapping of the breaking waves. I got up and cleared the table in two clean sweeps, gathered up the empty bottles, placed the glasses in the dishwasher and started it going. I stood motionless in the dimly lit kitchen for a while, gazing out at the embers of the fire.

On the smooth, black worktop lay the iPad. I opened the cover and made my way onto the webpages for planning and building work in the area. 'Report illegal building work', the link appeared at the bottom of the drop-down menu. I clicked on it. An opportunity for whistle-blowers who wanted to send their concerns anonymously. You only needed to provide the address and what it concerned, adding any images was voluntary.

A sound, I glanced out of the kitchen window. There was Kai, jogging up the steps, gleeful, a bottle in each hand. He stopped at the top of the steps and gazed around outside, looking confused to see everyone gone, before he caught sight of me inside.

I remained standing, holding his gaze. He disappeared

around the corner for a split second, before reappearing behind me, setting the bottles down on the kitchen island.

She's called it a night, he said, Hilma.

I thought as much, I replied. Per too.

Per? he said. Has Per left as well?

It's just the two of us now, I said, still with my back to him.

What are you doing? he asked.

I'm just looking at some pictures, I replied. I switched to the map app and put down the iPad, the orange rectangle on the satellite view glowing in the darkness. I gently slid the iPad towards him.

There wasn't a sound behind me at first, then I heard him swallow.

So? I said.

It became such a mess, he said. All of it. I was just trying to protect you. That time at the bar, when we ran into her – the colour drained from your face, you should have seen it. But she didn't recognise me.

I stood motionless, listening, he took a step closer and put a hand on my shoulder.

I never thought we'd end up here.

Here?

Here, in this cabin. I built this damn kitchen. Three years

ago! he exclaimed, kicking a cupboard so hard a drawer immediately popped open. It was the freezer drawer.

I said nothing, just grabbed the bottle of vodka and placed it on the counter with a thud.

Say something, he said.

I could see it now, this whole kitchen radiated Kai, it screamed his name down to the smallest detail.

So that thing you said about the height of the roof, I said, without turning around, that was true?